As he lowered his head, she whispered, "Marshall, please don't."

"Stop thinking for once. Just for one minute… feel…me."

His kiss was as tender and coaxing as his words, his lips brushing hers before skimming over to her cheek and chin, then back to her mouth. With slightly more pressure, he parted her lips. Genevieve tried to stop him again by touching her fingers to his mouth, but he only took hold of her hand and kissed each fingertip. All the while his gaze held hers. He could see as well as feel and hear his growing effect on her—the way her eyes dilated and her breath grew shallow, and the way she began to lose herself in what was happening between them.

"*Genevieve.* I could say your name all night. I want to." She felt unbelievable fitted against him—but she wasn't totally willing to be swept away. Although she let her eyelids drift closed, seduced by his caresses, her fingers sought and gripped at his shirt.

"Kiss me back," he coaxed. "Let go and wrap your arms around me. Hold me like I'm holding you. Need me like I'm needing you."

Dear Reader,

Welcome to Oak Point, Texas, and Lake Starling, not untypical of small northeast Texas towns where the tourism draw is countless lakes, miles of woods and forests, communities that know they need to grow—but not too much—and there's enough new blood arriving to keep life interesting.

As far as I could determine, there is no Oak Point, or Lake Starling, but you'll read about neighboring towns and businesses that do exist. Marshall stays at Oaklea Mansion and Manor House—that's definitely a landmark in Winnsboro, Texas. You can enjoy photos of this celebrity-favorite bed-and-breakfast online at www.oakleamansion.com to help you picture this serene and inspiring area. Mistra's is also an actual restaurant in the Hilton at Rockwall, Texas.

Now, Genevieve and Marshall weren't easy characters to write. Both have lost their spouses. One hasn't really recovered from that blow. The other is honestly relieved that a painful journey is over, and is ready to move on. What a challenge it is when, having found what he wants, she isn't ready for him. But life always has a way of intervening.

I hope you'll enjoy Genevieve and Marshall's journey of the heart. And please look for future releases at my Web site, www.helenrmyers.com.

As always, thank you for being a reader!

With warmest regards,

Helen R. Myers

IT STARTED WITH A HOUSE....

HELEN R. MYERS

SPECIAL EDITION

Published by Silhouette Books

America's Publisher of Contemporary Romance

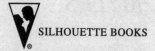

SILHOUETTE BOOKS

ISBN-13: 978-0-373-65552-6

Recycling programs
for this product may
not exist in your area.

IT STARTED WITH A HOUSE....

Visit Silhouette Books at www.eHarlequin.com

Printed in U.S.A.

HELEN R. MYERS

is a collector of two- and four-legged strays, and lives deep in the Piney Woods of East Texas. She cites cello music and bonsai gardening as favorite relaxation pastimes, and still edits in her sleep—an accident, learned while writing her first book. A bestselling author of diverse themes and focus, she is a three-time RITA® Award nominee, winning for *Navarrone* in 1993.

Prologue

"Marshall, we don't have to do this today," Genevieve Gale said the moment the dark-haired, gaunt-faced man exited the hospital and got into her silver Cadillac Escalade. "Under these circumstances, we can postpone for a week, more if necessary. The Carsons are proud to have you and Cynthia buying their house and they're compassionate and understanding people. They feel terrible that you feel obligated to continue with the closing today."

"These circumstances" were that Marshall Trent Roark's thirty-eight-year-old wife, Cynthia, had been admitted to the hospital here in Oak Point, Texas, two days ago, shortly after their drive up from Dallas. It would possibly be her last time at *any* medical facility, what with her battle with lung cancer almost over. Now her condition was compromised by pneumonia. It was the worst day possible to be holding a closing on a house.

"Cyn insisted." Adjusting his tan sports jacket that he

wore over a white polo shirt and jeans, Marshall busied himself with fastening his seat belt. "And it's not like I can do anything else. Hell, the doctors can't do anything except try to keep her as comfortable as possible. At least I can get this done. She thinks if I'm settled in at the new house, she can stop worrying about me. Isn't that a joke?" As he dropped his head back against the seat's headrest, he uttered a soul-weary sigh.

To Genevieve, he looked as if he hadn't slept a solid three hours in months, perhaps years. Chances were that he hadn't. Fresh from a shower, his black hair glistened as his determined movements made it fall over a high, but increasingly lined forehead that had nothing to do with age and everything to do with stress. His raw-boned face was freshly shaved, but there were dark shadows under his eyes and the corners of his sensual but compressed mouth seemed permanently turned down, a further sign of how tightly under control he was keeping himself. When they'd first met back in the spring, Genevieve had thought him physically striking, but a bit reticent, even aloof; however, she'd soon learned that wasn't his character at all. She had quickly learned that he was simply a man overwhelmed by life's turn of events, and was trying to cope as best as he could. It might be a beautiful August day at the northwest edge of Lake Starling, one of East Texas's prettiest private lakes, but you couldn't tell it by looking at him. Marshall looked strapped in for his millionth ride through purgatory, instead of what should have been one of the happier and exciting days of his and Cynthia's lives.

"Was it like this for you?" he asked after a prolonged silence.

Genevieve's grip on the steering wheel tightened as she dealt with the deeply personal question. She was often reluctant to discuss the loss of her husband with family or friends, first because it was all she had left of Adam and she protected that meager thing with almost rabid selfishness. Second because she hated what she saw on people's faces the few times she did answer. Sharing such feelings with a client put her in a gray area, and Genevieve tried to steer clear of such terrain and the complications that could result without them meaning to. Yet this was lining up to be one of those exception-to-the-rule moments in a break-all-rules association.

"Adam was a soldier and died overseas," she said of her late husband. "I didn't have to endure watching him slowly wither away before my eyes like you are with Cynthia."

That drew Marshall's scrutiny. "At least we've had the chance—maybe too many chances—to say goodbye. You didn't."

"No." What she wouldn't share was that Adam hadn't even let her come to the airport to see him off. He'd said that if she was there, he might not have been able to make himself board the plane this time. "Besides," he'd added, "I want to remember how you look lying here in our bed, naked and dreamy-eyed from me making love to you. Gen, I hope I've made you pregnant. Write me as soon as you know, okay?"

Genevieve shook her head, needing to block that particular memory. It was way too intimate and precious to share even with a friend. And even though it was now almost four years and the raw pain of his loss had healed to a sensitive scar, the reality was that sometimes the simple act of breathing remained a trial for her.

"I'm sorry," Marshall said when he saw her swallow two, then three times. "I had no right."

She uttered a brief, broken sound that was neither laugh nor protest, yet somehow gave her the oxygen to say a little more. "If anyone does, it's you. All I do know is that you're about to join a club that no one wants to belong to. There are no words to change it or make it easier. All you can do is deal with things one click of the clock at a time." *Until you think you'll go mad,* she continued to herself, *or lose the ability to think altogether, or you wish for your heart to quit beating altogether because of sheer exhaustion.*

As Genevieve exited the hospital's property, she joined the heavier morning traffic on Main Street. Oak Point was a six-traffic-light town and it wouldn't take more than five minutes to get to the title company. She'd insisted on picking him up because she'd kept on top of Cynthia's status and anticipated his emotional state and the exhaustion that came with it. He didn't need to be behind the wheel of a car even for a few minutes.

As though reading her mind, Marshall glanced at her again and said, "You do know that we're both eternally grateful to you, don't you? You've been gracious and patient, and too kind. You've made this as easy as anyone could."

The quietly spoken sentiments, as much as the sadness that underscored them, had Genevieve briefly touching her hand to her heart and made her eyes burn. "Thank you, but stop. Anyone would have been grateful for the opportunity to be your agent and help you. You and Cynthia are wonderful people and Oak Point needs you."

"Maybe, but you've become a friend, Genevieve—and you know I've had enough real estate dealings to accept that doesn't often happen."

"Then I'm doubly glad you think so, too," she said just as softly. She had intended to say something similar to him and Cynthia jointly after the closing, and to hear Marshall speak the words first filled her with a unique, yet bittersweet joy. Heavens, at this rate, she was going to be openly crying in a minute, and so she attempted to redirect their conversation to practical matters that might have slipped by the wayside due to unmitigated circumstances. "So speaking as a friend, have you confirmed the arrival time of your movers?"

"The truck should be arriving tomorrow morning by 8:30. Heaven knows where I'm supposed to tell them to put everything, let alone deal with the unpacking when I need to be at the hospital."

Genevieve began to reply, hesitated, and then ventured, "I remember quite a bit of what Cynthia said about how she would like the living room to look. The dining area is a given due to its shape and the shape of your table. We could temporarily guess about the bedroom. Would you like me to come over and give you a hand?"

Marshall's expression reflected a man torn between hope and conscience. "You can't possibly have the time. I know for a fact that you've already devoted way too many hours to us because of—Cyn's deteriorating condition."

Those hours had cultivated deeper feelings and gained her broader insights into the Roarks' lives, and Genevieve knew that Marshall had no one else to call on for help. Both he and Cynthia had been only children—or that was what had been eluded—and Cynthia's parents were in California, but estranged from her, while Marshall's were deceased. There might be extended family and un- doubtedly friends in Dallas that they could reach out to; however, Marshall never brought up the prospect.

"I have a morning appointment that isn't critical," Genevieve told him. "If you'd like, I'll reschedule as soon as I get back to the office. If the truck arrives as promised, we should have you in good shape by noon or not long thereafter."

With sculpted fingers, Marshall raked back his wavy, maestro-long hair. "You keep leaving me speechless, Genevieve. Having been in the restaurant business almost half of my life, I know more than a little about Southern hospitality and the wisdom in stroking customers and pampering clients, but you put me to shame."

Struggling not to take too much personal pleasure out of his appreciation, she reached for her reliable prag- matism. Granted, the change in plans would delay her catching up on other deals in progress, but she would worry about Marshall coping with trying to be in two places at once anyway. Then there was Cynthia lying in the hospital feeling perhaps afraid or abandoned. Forc- ing a brighter smile, Genevieve quipped, "We have more churches per capita than you do in Dallas. Our ministers would lay on the fire-and-brimstone sermons really thick if they heard you weren't being treated right as a new resident of Oak Point."

However, once she parked in front of the title com- pany, Genevieve turned to Marshall. "My conscience demands I give you another chance to table this. Say the word and we'll reschedule."

"No." Although undeniably fatigued, Marshall reached for the door handle. "Cynthia was struggling to stay conscious waiting on the news that the house was ours. Let's get this done."

His confession had another, harder knot of dread forming in her abdomen. She exited her vehicle, opening the back to retrieve her leather shoulder bag. The honey tint matched her high heels. She discreetly smoothed her long blond hair, then the slim skirt of her camel-colored suit. At least, she thought, slamming the door and joining him on the sidewalk, this was a cash deal and the paperwork would be minimal.

Once inside the white-brick title company, Genevieve warmly greeted the four middle-aged ladies who owned and operated the business. As she introduced Marshall, she wasn't surprised that they became like teenage girls in the presence of a school heartthrob. She couldn't blame them. Like a bird of prey, Marshall Roark's face possessed a fearsome beauty that drew the eye; however, the rest of the man deserved equal admiration. He was tall and sinewy rather than muscular, which gave his movements an elegance, enhanced by long legs and slim hips. The ladies offered him everything but wine, phone numbers and a room key. Genevieve observed their reactions with a mixture of bemusement and sympathy since, like her, one of the women was widowed, two divorced and the other's husband was on the run for legal reasons. Nevertheless, as sad as Genevieve was for the lonely women, she was more concerned for her client's comfort. She'd called ahead to warn the ladies of

Marshall's increasingly grim situation to avoid questions about Cynthia, and she diplomatically guided him into the meeting room where they could get on with things.

It took less than a half hour. The legal issues and paperwork had long been resolved. At Cynthia's insistence, the house was going to be in Marshall's name alone. Marshall was paying cash for the five-thousand-square-foot structure set on three acres. The house was already vacated by the Carsons, who'd retired to Arizona to be closer to their grandchildren. Actually, Genevieve's work was done, except to confirm that the inspector's documentation was all in order, the utilities had been transferred—and to stand by and get Marshall out of there should he suddenly decide he couldn't go through with this, after all. But having also bought and sold several office buildings in the DFW area, along with a chain of restaurants, he was the real veteran in the room and managed the transaction with greater professionalism and dignity than she could have if the tables were turned.

At the end, he shook hands with Marti Quinn and thanked her for her efficiency and kindness. His deep, brushed-velvet voice had Marti blushing anew. Genevieve wasn't immune herself. Not in the least. If it wasn't for her constant consciousness of Cynthia, she would be well on her way toward having a crush herself—and that was saying a great deal for her.

Thanking Marti for the check that the older woman handed her, which represented her commission as agent and broker, Genevieve escorted Marshall out of the building.

They weren't halfway down the sidewalk when Marshall's BlackBerry buzzed. A half-step ahead of him,

Genevieve glanced over and their gazes collided. Clearly, he hadn't been expecting a call—or maybe he had and anticipated the worst?

Taking a step back, she touched his arm. "You have to answer it," she said gently.

Grim-faced, he drew out the device, took one look at the screen and flexed his strong jaw.

That expression told her all that she needed to know. "Give me those and I'll get the Escalade's doors unlocked." She took his folder of closing papers from him and left him the modicum of privacy that was available.

Lowering his head, Marshall connected and said, "Roark." After a moment, he said, "Tell me."

Genevieve triggered her key and opened the passenger door to the SUV, which had less to do with saving him from the vehicle's interior heat and everything to do with the prospect of more privacy if he realized he needed it. Then she circled toward the back, stealing glimpses of him around corners and through glass on her way to the driver's side. Regardless of her undeniable attraction to the man, she owed him her protection and support. Her intuition told her to get as far away from him as possible, away from what this phone call might set into motion. Her sense of responsibility made that impossible.

Marshall suddenly turned his back to her. She drew in a sharp breath and began preparing herself for the worst in that strange way the mind functioned, even when you consciously were rejecting what was happening. He set his left hand on his hip and tilted his head back to look up at the cloudless sky. A 747 was descending on its approach into DFW airport, some hundred miles west.

Genevieve could have bet what was left of her heart that he didn't see it. As tension in his squared shoulders tested the silk of his tailored jacket, she wished there was something she could do, but she knew from experience that if this was as bad as she feared, for the moment any presence whatsoever was unwelcome.

She got into the driver's seat of the Escalade and, after keying the engine to cool down the vehicle, stared at the steering wheel, then out the driver's window, anywhere to give him some semblance of privacy. Just as she gave up and let her gaze return to him, he disconnected. Gripping the BlackBerry as though trying to decide whether to crush it or fling it to heaven—or hell—he came to the SUV and climbed in. That was all. He didn't try to close the door or fasten his seat belt, he just sat there.

Genevieve turned down the blowers two notches so he could hear her. "Marshall, close the door," she coaxed. "I'll get you back there."

He turned to her, his dark blue eyes an unforgettable combination of shock and pain.

"It's too late," he said. "She's already gone."

Chapter One

Cynthia Kittredge Roark's death put any thought of a moving day onto the back burner of Marshall's life. Instead, he escorted his wife's body back to Northern California, where it was reported she was to be laid to rest in the Kittredge family mausoleum.

It was another two weeks before Genevieve heard from Marshall again. Upon his return, he called from the bed-and-breakfast Oaklea Mansion and Manor House in the nearby piney woods town of Winnsboro where he'd been staying whenever he and Cynthia had driven in from Dallas. He asked Genevieve if her offer still stood to help him get situated. Genevieve didn't hesitate; she assured him that he only had to give her a day and time and she would arrange to be at the Lake Starling house.

The movers finally appeared four days later. Concerned by the extra time the place had sat empty,

Genevieve arranged for—with Marshall's blessing—a thorough cleaning using the reliable service she employed herself, as did her mother. By the time the massive eighteen-wheeler backed onto the cement driveway on the third Friday in August bearing the Roarks' furniture and personal belongings, she was able to direct them through a house that sparkled in welcome.

Thank goodness another early morning delivery had been possible. By eight o'clock, the temperatures had already climbed beyond the overnight eighty-three degrees despite the supposed cooling lake breeze. At least the new double-door stainless-steel refrigerator was in place and the electricity was on. The ice machine was up to speed, and Genevieve—using a key that Marshall had left with her—had one shelf stocked since the previous afternoon with bottled water and soft drinks for the crew, which she pointed out to them before they started unloading.

She had dressed partly for a day of labor, determined to make things as easy as possible for Marshall, but wasn't quite able to give up on her need to be prepared for an office emergency. Her jeans were the ones she saved for attic filter changes and the serious refrigerator cleaning, her sneakers the same ones she used at the gym. But her gauzy caramel-colored top was dressier. She'd brushed her shoulder-length blond hair into a no-nonsense ponytail, yet her gold hoop earrings were unmistakably the real thing. In the Escalade were stylish heels and a white cotton blazer that could get her ready for a sudden business meeting within minutes if the need arrived.

With her clipboard in hand, her BlackBerry clipped

to it, and her own bottle of water on the black-speckled quartz breakfast bar, Genevieve was ready for whatever the day would throw at her. What she *hoped* was that her staff would be able to handle anything that surfaced back at the office, so that she could get Marshall somewhat set up with the bare essentials before too late in the afternoon. That would mean having to work more overtime at the office in order not to fall behind with her other clients, but it was something she wanted as much as felt a need to do.

From the beginning, well before the Carsons had listed this house, it had been a favorite of hers among the luxury lake houses. The design was a mix of modern and contemporary, a gray-speckled brick, the focal point being the family/great room that was enhanced by a partial second story of lead-glass windows and a giant fireplace to provide both light under almost any weather conditions and warmth throughout the house. More lead-glass windows looked out to a wrap-around porch, an open-tiled courtyard in back, and beyond that a covered peninsula that faced the lake, pier and boathouse. The country kitchen was state-of-the-art, the elegant counters echoing the shimmering outside brick, and a copper stove hood added dramatic contrast. The split-bedrooms design featured a huge master suite, and on the other side of the house were three other bedrooms. A formal dining room and sizable office with many built-ins rounded out the main floor plan.

It was a house for professional or active people and perfect for entertaining; nevertheless, it was still a thousand square feet smaller than her mother's residence located two properties to the right. What concerned

Genevieve was that Marshall's house was undeniably large for one person, particularly someone newly grieving with no one close to help him through the first rough weeks and months.

Although he was on the premises, Marshall had made it clear that he would be grateful to hold to their previous agreement that she handle most of the decisions and issue the directives as to what was put where. His trust was the highest form of flattery; however, Genevieve worried that he'd bestowed her that authority simply because he no longer cared. Was that reflective of the house itself, himself or both?

As the master bedroom furnishings began to be unloaded, Genevieve saw him sitting on the back patio wall, his BlackBerry in hand. He wasn't talking or texting, he was simply staring off across the lake. She remembered that pose well from her early days after Adam's death and knew if Marshall was able to think at all, he was wondering if his mind would ever function reliably again. Only he could resolve his "alone" and "now what?" issues. Thankfully, decisions about the rest of his life didn't have to be made today. As for the unpacking, Genevieve reasoned that if he decided to put the place back on the market, it would show much better if it was furnished. Secretly, she couldn't keep from hoping he would give the house—and Oak Point—a chance.

Throughout the morning, she stayed busy with the movers. While she had kitchen boxes stacked on the counters and in the huge pantry, and boxes marked "Marshall—bedroom" and "linens" delivered to the master suite, she had everything with Cynthia's name delivered to the first bedroom on the west side of the house. In between answering questions from the supervisor named Benny, she found the boxes that would initially allow Marshall to make coffee, and eat off something besides paper plates and drink out of glass and porcelain instead of plastic.

When the workers were done in the master suite, she found a box of linens to make sure Marshall had a bed ready to sleep in and towels for his bathroom. She had to resort to her own "emergency" bag of brought-along supplies to finish things. They included essentials like bathroom tissue, soap, toothpaste and shampoo to keep him well stocked for several days.

Whether it was the heat or guilt, eventually Marshall came inside and attempted to show some interest in how things were coming along. He was astounded at her progress in the master suite, but when he spotted Cynthia's boxes in the other bedroom, the look he shot her almost broke her heart. Right after that he retreated to the office and closed the door. Genevieve managed not to interrupt him again until the desk and file cabinets were ready to be placed in there.

And then it was done. Once she signed the paperwork and handed Benny the tip Marshall had provided, she made sure he and his men took more refreshments for their return trip to Dallas and waved them off.

The sound of the big diesel engine rumbling back to life brought Marshall from some remote part of the house and he joined her in the kitchen. With an understanding smile, she pointed to the receipts on the counter. "Mission accomplished—and without too much damage. There's a table scratch, which can probably be rubbed out, but I made them initial for it here—" she pointed to the appropriate page "—and for a chip out of the bed's headboard." She pointed to the second initial.

"Those are both my fault, not theirs," Marshall said.

Genevieve nodded, experience allowing her to read between the lines. She, too, had been grateful for everyone's kindness and help during her darkest days, but there came a time when she began wishing that she lived in a bigger city that would provide anonymity because she didn't think she could bear even one more pitying or curious look, or "chin up, life goes on" lecture. At her lowest point, she'd lived to get home and release some of that pressure.

"I broke a clock against our fireplace mantel," she confessed. She added a sheepish smile. "Frankly, it was the ugliest wedding gift we'd received, and I wasn't sorry to see it go. I'll give the company a call immediately and tell them that the notations are nonissues."

"The headboard happened right after we contracted on this place and I caught Cynthia sneaking a cigarette," Marshall said with equal chagrin. "I was frustrated and angry. I threw a gift, too. A silver picture frame. I'll handle the call, Genevieve."

Wedding photos were often in silver frames, she thought. Hers were. For weeks after Adam's death, she couldn't bear to see a photo of him without falling apart and for a while had put them facedown, until seeing them that way would make her feel guilty so she would place them upright again, until she had to hide them behind books and in drawers because it hurt too much to look at his dear face. But she'd never wanted to throw a photo of him. The box containing his flag maybe, because she'd been as angry with the military as she'd been with the radical militants who'd killed him. The thing was that being a soldier had been in his blood and she'd married him knowing that. Wasn't it the same for Marshall with Cynthia? From what they'd told her, they'd met in college and she'd been a near life-long smoker.

"Okay, then…" Realizing that she had no more reason to stay, Genevieve tucked her pen into her bag and pulled out something from the bottom of the clipboard that she'd worked up for him. "Well, the good news is that you can take your time from here on. Here's a sheet with service phone numbers."

"I told you that you were incredible. The gift that keeps on giving," he murmured.

His admiring gaze had her feeling as if she was one step away from blushing. Determined to keep to her professional script, she focused on the paper she passed to him. "A simple printout of what I already have in the computer. These are people we hire repeatedly at the office and you can feel free to use my name, although by now everyone knows yours, so you probably won't have any trouble getting quick service. Also your address is a dead giveaway."

"Does that mean I should tip them double? Not that I mind if they're as good as you say," Marshall added with a shrug, "but I don't want to immediately become the hated one on the street by the rest of my neighbors."

Those neighbors included her mother, a fact that he had been informed of back when he and Cynthia first looked at the house. "If I recommend someone, you can pretty much trust that you won't be dealing with padded invoices, so tip as you see fit."

Placing the paper on top of the receipt, he shoved his hands into the pockets of his jeans. "How do I thank you? You've gone above and beyond what I intended or imagined."

"Full disclosure time—fun for me is playing decorator, and I have the best job to feed that because I get to see so many styles and ideas. The muscle boys had the hard work." Seeing the new potential in the place, she tried to infuse him with a little of her excitement. "Do you like it so far?" What Genevieve really wanted to ask was, *"Do you think you could consider staying despite what's happened?"*

"What's not to like?" Marshall replied. "It's a fabulous house and you've done the most with what you had to work with. In bad weather, I can even jog using the wrap-around patio. With luck, I can crack open my skull slipping on sweating concrete and quit worrying about what I'm supposed to do with myself here alone."

"Marshall." His last words shook her almost as much as when he took that awful call weeks ago outside of the title company. Genevieve couldn't keep from fingering the delicate gold cross her paternal grandmother had given her at her christening. Loss that cut soul-deep opened one to so many dangers.

He held up his hand to entreat her patience. "I'm being a self-pitying jerk. Ignore me, please. I'm used to knowing immediately what to do when and the protocol involved. I could arrange for dinner for a surprise visit by a foreign dignitary or celebrity with barely any notice, but right now just this small talk with you is almost making me break out in a cold sweat."

She understood completely. "Then I should leave."

"Don't. I mean, I wish you wouldn't."

Having started to reach for her things, Genevieve hesitated. "But you just said—"

"What I meant was that I was editing myself mute. It's been a progressive thing…mostly to avoid conflict with Cynthia, because getting upset was the last thing she needed given her prognosis. Increasingly, I've found the tendency is bleeding into the other parts of my life."

The admission that Cynthia was so addicted to nicotine that even when on oxygen she would light up was bad enough; Genevieve couldn't begin to imagine how difficult it was for Marshall—trying to help her when she would not or could not be helped. "I must admit when we first met, I thought you a bit difficult to read, but I soon concluded that was simply your desire for privacy, combined with your first-rate professionalism."

Marshall looked away and rubbed his nape. "Bless you. At least now you know how wrong you are."

"No, I don't think so."

When he looked back at her, he shook his head and smiled. Although it was a sad smile, it was the first time she saw something close to a natural reaction from him— other than one of pain—and the tenderness of it almost took her breath away. He had a face that made her think of brooding Irish poets and brave Greek gods, nothing like today's air-brushed cover-model perfect images, but a face full of character and intelligence earned by some life-altering bumps and blows along the way. Suddenly she saw a new layer of the charisma that he was capable of, and Genevieve was grateful to have the counter to hold on to. Combined with his penetrating eyes, she felt almost as weak-kneed as one of her mother's fictional heroines.

"Oh, hell," he muttered and tore his gaze away only to gesture to the refrigerator. "I saw that generous gift of champagne you sneakily tucked in the back of everything. At least stay long enough to join me in a glass?"

"You weren't supposed to notice it until I left," Genevieve replied, trying to figure out all that was going on beneath the surface of the man as fast as he hid it. "As a matter of fact, I debated not putting it there at all. It's a given that you don't feel like celebrating—"

"Well, if you leave without sharing a glass with me, it's apt to still be in there when you next put the house on the market."

He didn't seem to say that as a threat, just a fact of life, but the fact that it was a possibility triggered a sinking feeling inside her. Against her better judgment, she found herself reaching for her BlackBerry. "Let me take this outside and check my messages and see how things are at the office. One glass," she added as she backed toward the French doors leading to the patio. "I haven't eaten enough today to risk more and can't afford to be seen driving off the culvert at the end of your driveway. Juice glasses in the upper cabinet to the right of the sink." She pointed. "That and the ice tea size are all that's unpacked so far."

Genevieve always enjoyed the view of the lake and this early-afternoon image was of smooth-glass perfection. It helped to soothe the nerves playing havoc with her body and psyche. She should have left as soon as Marshall had thanked her. The fact that he hadn't needed to try hard to make her linger told her that she was behaving way out of her norm and needed a reality check. Fast.

Unless she was beyond clueless, Marshall Roark was attracted to her. But he was apparently as troubled by that as she was startled by her own attraction to him. She reminded herself that sexual awareness so soon following such a loss was common. She'd experienced it herself, only the men who'd made passes hadn't been anyone she could be remotely attracted to. She'd yearned only for Adam. However, that didn't stop the sleepless nights, and days of compromised focus due to her libido, so how could she be offended or judge Marshall, even though Cynthia wasn't gone a full month yet?

On the other hand, she'd been alone four years now and thought she'd perfected keeping an invisible barrier between herself and unwanted male attention. That just proved how good Marshall was at undermining her resolve. She would have to be extracareful—not only when she got back inside, but in the future.

Inwardly shaking her head at this potential emotional maelstrom, Genevieve called the office. Her senior agent Avery Pageant answered. "How are things going?" she asked.

"Ina and I are holding the fort," the forty-two-year-old divorcée replied. "She's in the kitchen getting our lunches ready. We're both eating late today to avoid dinner. Raenne is off showing the Cook farm."

"Did she have her boots and gun with her when she left?"

"Yes, Mommy."

The friendly taunt didn't offend Genevieve. They were a close group and although she was the youngest in the

office—with Raenne thirty-five, and Ina thirty-three—
they all understood that, as the broker, Genevieve was
key to the reputation and soundness of the business. They
also knew there was a huge difference between showing
lakefront property and a good-size farm with creeks and
wildlife. Often that wildlife was of the deadly variety.
Then there was the matter of who was asking to see such
property. Raenne was married, but you couldn't tell it
by her redneck husband, who would travel three or five
states for a bass tournament yet wouldn't act as backup
to his wife when she showed large tracts of land. It was
left to Genevieve to remind her staff to be cautious; only
last year a female agent a few towns away had been
murdered showing property—and that had occurred in
a development!

"What about your afternoon appointment?" she asked
Avery. "Is that still on?"

"No, the couple found out they won't get the financing
for that much house. At least they didn't waste my time.
I'll hunt them something more in their price range and
get back to them."

"Good for you. All right, I'm planning on being back
there within the hour."

Genevieve had just disconnected when she heard the
French doors open behind her. Listening to Marshall's
footsteps as he approached, she pointed across the cove
at the cedar two-story partially hidden by seventy-year-
old pines. "It looks like one of your on-the-road-again
neighbors is back in town."

"Beau Stanton the singer, right?" Marshall stopped
beside her and handed her one of the glasses. "Based out
of Nashville, I believe you said."

As the small caravan consisting of a sparkling top-of-the-line pickup truck, a cargo van and two SUVs of equal quality parked on the driveway, Genevieve nodded. "That's the one. Those pricey black vehicles almost resemble a presidential entourage, don't they?"

"They don't look quite as bulletproof."

"Of course. There's that." And Marshall would know better than she would given his background of hobnobbing with the rich and famous. Worried that she might have sounded as if she was showing off, Genevieve grew silent.

"Didn't you tell me that he had the walls of his house built with extra insulation and the windows specially designed so that he won't irritate neighbors during rehearsals and jam sessions? Considerate of him," Marshall said, "although I wouldn't mind hearing a tune or two now and again."

"Not at three or four in the morning you wouldn't. When musicians jam, they're not aware of the time. He loves it here," Genevieve said, finally turning. She knew what Marshall had done to make her feel comfortable, and thought him all the more a gentleman for it. "The lake has become a creative inspiration to him, so, like you, he's determined not to create any bad blood with his neighbors." She nodded with simple admiration. "You're kind to overlook my ignorance and you paid excellent attention when I first showed you the place."

He touched his glass to hers. "In the end, it's all in the details, isn't it?"

"I can't argue with that," she murmured, once again wondering what else he was implying. After taking a necessary sip of the delicious vintage, Genevieve dove, perhaps too eagerly, into a reminder of who else he shared the deep cove with—bankers, retired sports stars, a world-renowned surgeon and her mother in the Mediterranean-style those two properties over. On their first tour of this home, with her typical full disclosure style, she'd made him and Cynthia fully aware of the familial connection. Cynthia had suffered a frightening coughing-choking fit at the news.

"You're kidding me? I love her work!" she'd declared. "If she could write faster, she might get me to give up cigarettes."

Marshall hadn't been amused at his wife's dark humor, considering her already fragile health, but Genevieve had eased the moment by promising that she would let her mother know and would get any books she wanted autographed. Sadly, that had remained a commitment unfulfilled.

Genevieve glanced toward the Texas version of a villa and hoped her mother wasn't watching with her military-power binoculars from her second-story office. A tight publishing deadline was the only safe time Genevieve could be showing in the area and not be spotted without getting an immediate text message demanding, "*Who* is that?" When she'd first spotted Marshall Roark, Sydney had texted, "Who is *that?*"

"I've lost you," Marshall said. "Is something wrong?"

"Can we go back inside?" Genevieve asked and began leading the way. "I'm afraid that if my mother catches sight of us standing here, she'll invite herself over."

"Ah, yes. I seem to remember you referring to her as 'part bloodhound and part shark.'"

"She's as environmentally efficient as the latter, too.

Just about everything she sniffs out information-wise will end up in one of her novels. For someone who values his privacy, you'll want to remember that."

"You sound like you've been nipped a time or two." Marshall's long strides helped him beat her to the door and open it for her.

"Let's just say you won't find many Genevieves in East Texas. My namesake happened to be a character that she became so enthralled with, she couldn't resist naming me that, as well. It helped being born forty-eight hours after she finished that manuscript."

"It's a beautiful name," he replied. "So the Genevieve-based character was someone your mother had met before?"

"Who had enough tragedy in her life to become a book. Don't bother asking me for the title," Genevieve replied.

"You tempt me, but I'll resist for now." Marshall tilted his head as they paused at the bar. "You can't see that the name suits you?"

"No more than *Gigi* does. That's G.G., my married initials. Mother thought a character called Gabrielle Gallant was enough disguise to turn the most recent and painful chapters of *my* life into fiction, as well. The rest is another bit of *New York Times*–list history."

"Ah. Ouch. Now I'm beginning to understand," Marshall replied thoughtfully. His look was sympathetic. "So you two aren't speaking? Excuse me—now I'm trespassing on *your* privacy."

With a fatalistic shrug, Genevieve took a last sip of champagne and made herself set the half-full glass on the counter. "We speak. I've resigned myself to the reality that she's incorrigible and, when she blithely shares her latest tromp into my life or the lives of others that I know and care about, she accepts that I need to avoid her calls for a day or a week, depending on the offense."

"You've opened my eyes to a different perspective. It's one thing to see print page opinions or the headlines from the news portrayed on TV dramas a month after the fact, but I'm realizing it's not so entertaining when it's your own history in novel form." Marshall continued, "Would I be getting too personal if I asked if Sawyer is your maiden name?"

Genevieve tucked her BlackBerry into her bag. "Not at all. Charles Sawyer was my father. He died in a tractor accident when I was fifteen. As sad as that sounds, he was looking over some new land he'd just purchased. I guess I inherited his love of land. Mother's current husband is Bart—short for Barton—Conway. Part saint, part Saint Bernard, not always tolerant of Mother's shenanigans, but faithful, reliable, all of the qualities one needs with a high-maintenance wife like Sydney. They're working on their tenth anniversary. My hunch is that he'll stick. My *prayer* is he'll stick. Between him and Dad was Whit. Whitfield Edwards. You won't hear that name spoken unless there's an obituary notice. Not Mother's," Genevieve intoned.

"Was theirs a bad experience partially due to things happening too soon after your father's death?"

Pointing her index finger at him, she replied, "Bingo. For a time, Mother did consider the working title *The Expensive Case of Rebound* but she never wrote the book… or learned from the experience. She started dating Bart at an investments seminar two weeks after her divorce was final."

"Sometimes it happens quickly for some people," Marshall said, gesturing with his glass.

Genevieve shook her head. "You can't be interested in any of this."

"I actually believe in seminars. The results from several have kept me from firing a few employees." When Genevieve failed to respond to that, he added, "What does Saint Bart do while your mother is writing? I didn't see a boathouse, so I'm guessing he's not a fisherman."

"The only water Bart is interested in comes from his shower head or is the frozen kind—ice in his scotch. He likes golf, poker and the online link to his stock trader." Genevieve pointed to the notes she'd left him. "Don't forget the security people will be out tomorrow to check on your system and recommend upgrades."

"Thanks. Should I make a point to introduce myself to the police chief?"

"Phil Irvine. I asked him to stop by in the next few days, but you're right, it wouldn't hurt to initiate the meeting yourself. He's a good man. His son is a talented junior on the high school football team and already being watched by college scouts. His elder child, a daughter, died in a wreck last year. I'm only offering that because Phil can be a bit gruff these days. Please don't take it personally."

Marshall stayed her hand as she reached for her bag. "Do you ever stop working?"

His unexpected touch made it difficult to think, let alone answer. "I'm only trying to help make this impossible situation—"

"Easier. You have. But, Genevieve, do you think you could go off the clock now and just talk to me?"

She knew she should have resisted the champagne. So that intuition about his attraction had been dead-on, but while her heart skipped a beat in ridiculous pleasure, her mind—ever the devil's advocate—was fast to hoist walls. "Oh, Marshall…you know that's not a good idea."

"Then you realize that I don't want to talk about my neighbors or your family, I want to talk about you."

She kept her gaze on the hand slowly clasping hers. "Yes."

"What if I asked you to dinner?"

"You shouldn't."

"Because there's someone already in your life?"

The easy way out would be to say, "Yes," but that would be lying. However, she gently extricated herself and looped her bag over her shoulder. "Marshall…I'm flattered. Truly. And what you think you're feeling is normal after suffering such a huge loss, but it's not—"

"Don't say 'real.' Not only isn't this a temporary aberration, I was attracted to you the moment I saw your photo on the realty Web site. When I actually met you, I was relieved that Cynthia shook your hand first because I needed a moment to collect myself."

His admission was everything a woman wanted to hear from a man she also felt an attraction to—only Genevieve wasn't proud of having those feelings about the husband of a woman she'd hoped would become a friend. "Please don't tell me that. Do you realize how bizarre that is? Cyn—"

"Had been ill for a considerable while, you know that. Genevieve—of all women I'd have expected you to understand. I was a faithful husband until we met you. I took my 'for better or worse' commitment seriously."

"I appreciate you sharing that," she replied. While she refused to let this get out of hand, she would hate for her image of him to be completely shattered.

"But you're still uneasy." Marshall stroked his thumb over her soft skin.

"Anyone would be."

"No, not anyone. You. You're far more decent and principled than many of your sex, Genevieve. Believe me, from my past vantage point, I've seen plenty." Then, with a faint smile, he added, "But I'm fairly certain that you blushed at least twice when I caught you looking at me."

Mortified, Genevieve pulled her hand free and covered her eyes. "Please tell me that Cynthia never saw that?"

"She didn't. But don't torment yourself. She liked you and would approve of this. Us."

"There is no us. It's just too soon." She gestured toward the French doors. "Besides which, I've established a nice business here. Gossip could destroy a reputation in my business as quickly as getting called up on ethics charges."

"What are we supposed to do, pretend we feel nothing until the police and local gossips give the signal that we've suffered enough to suit them?" Marshall uttered something disparaging under his breath. "Speaking for myself, I've been through several kinds of hell watching the slow death of my wife, and the slower death of my marriage due to our spats about her inability to quit smoking. I want to feel something besides pity, regret, grief and guilt. I *want* my life back."

Genevieve understood, sympathized and even agreed with him. In principle. But, while she wasn't a coward, she had to avert her eyes to protect herself from the intensity she knew was radiating in his. Marshall was a passionate man and she recognized that now that he was free and had made his feelings known, she was all the more vulnerable to him.

"Look at me," he ordered softly. When she failed to comply, he closed the short distance between them and put his fingers under her chin, forcing her to meet his gaze. "You know what? I think you're even more confused and trapped than I am by this world of cellophane morals and shredded principles, so this is what I'm going to do. I'm going to kiss you. Then you'll leave—probably as quickly as I'll want you to go, but for entirely different reasons. And we'll talk again after you've had a chance to really get used to the idea. Understand?"

She shook her head.

Marshall exhaled in a brief, low laugh. "God help me," he said, lowering his head. "Neither do I."

Chapter Two

For the next hour after Genevieve left, Marshall sat at his desk in his new office, his gaze on Genevieve Gale's business card from The Gale Agency. The colored photograph in the top left corner was flattering in that one-dimensional, photo-by-stranger way, but it didn't begin to do her justice. The photo he was wishing he had framed before him was one fresh in his mind—Genevieve just kissed.

His chest rose and fell on a deep breath as he sought the last nuance of her scent. She made him think of his first taste of lemon gelato years ago when he was fresh out of college and racing through Europe before he got too buried in his career. It had been refreshing and sexy, and addictive the way chocolate could be to others.

Closing his eyes, he relived how she'd stared at his mouth until just before his lips touched hers, then raised her gaze to seek further confirmation of the truth in his eyes. He knew she'd seen it because his emotions had his heartbeat nearly rupturing his eardrums, especially when she'd touched her fingers to his face in appeal—for what, he wasn't sure. To reconsider? To be sure he knew what he was doing? Coming this far, he couldn't have stopped if he'd wanted to, and he definitely didn't want to. He'd waited long enough for this.

Genevieve. Like her name, she was elegant and graceful. A lady. A fine businesswoman and a person anyone would want as a friend. But there was much more to the woman, and he wanted to explore the far reaches of her mind, just as he wanted to learn every inch of that body.

Afterward, she'd fled, pale, her caramel eyes strangely shadowed from the shock of her rediscovered passion, while her gently bowed lips were swollen from a kiss that had gone from whisper-soft to ardent before either of them could stop it. It thrilled him to discover she wasn't as in control as her professional demeanor suggested, and to learn that she wanted him, too. Granted, she would continue to struggle with this and feel guilt—hell, he did and would for some time himself. You couldn't live with another person for over a decade and a half and make every memory go away. Nevertheless, he was also grateful that he wouldn't have to endure the bar scene and blind dates that would have been his future. The woman he wanted wouldn't require a background search or blood test to prove her health status. Such a gift had to be treated with the utmost respect and care; however, having repressed his sexual craving for so long, he was like a parched creek bed ready to soak her up in one desperate swallow. It had been a challenge to let her go, and he was already wondering how long she would make him wait before he could see her again.

Marshall made himself get out of the leather chair and do another, more thorough, examination of the house. He was impressed with how well Genevieve remembered Cynthia's directives between draws at the oxygen mask of where she would put what. The furnishings seemed made for the house, a sturdy mix of leather and wood, the colors mostly earth tones with accents of green, egg-plant and blue. None of the paintings were hung yet, just a few of the knickknacks were unboxed, and only one lamp—a Frank Lloyd Wright type of design, the shade made of agates and quartz, the frame brass. It looked as if it had been made for the house, and Marshall wondered if Genevieve had placed it on the sofa table behind the couch where it was immediately a focal point, or was it simply the resting spot decided by one of the movers? Never. It had to have been Genevieve. Poor Cynthia had a mathematician's rather uninspired taste for decorating. If a lamp, ashtray or book was set on one end table, their twins had to be on the other. A wreath on one side of the door required a matching one on the other side. She was all about regimen and order, partly because of the way she grew up, partly because of losing her twin, Scott. Heaven knew he'd tried to figure it out and set her free to be more impulsive and experimental.

In contrast, Marshall could already see by the few pieces that Genevieve had unpacked that she avoided clutter, and wasn't afraid of mixing styles. He wondered what her home looked like. He wondered what else she could do with this place if given the opportunity.

That gave him an idea and, as he returned to the

kitchen, he reached for his BlackBerry and clicked on her number in his address book. For a moment he thought he would only get her voice mail, but then she was on the line saying hesitantly, "I didn't expect to hear from you again today."

"Am I pushing my luck?"

After a pause, Genevieve replied softly, "I have no right to say that—I kissed you back."

Reaching over to her wineglass, Marshall stroked his thumb over the hint of lipstick on the rim. "And left me wanting so much more."

Clearing her throat, Genevieve said, "Ina just signaled that I have a call holding and my least patient agent is about to barge into my office."

Taking the hint, Marshall made his point quickly. "I have an request, plea or whatever you want to call it. I've just finished going through the house to see all you did, and I'm stuck. I'm an administrator and idea guy. I can renovate a building and suggest an atmosphere that I'm going for, but I don't know anything about decorating until I see what I like."

"That sounds like an apology, not an request."

"Help."

There was another pause, then her weak, "You're not playing fair."

"Darling, I'm not playing at all. If you don't agree to help me, I'll have to hire a perfect stranger, and I don't want a stranger around, I want you. When you aren't driving me to distraction, you're a balm to my weary soul."

"You seem to be overlooking that I have a job."

"Not at all. This could be lunch dates, dinner dates

and getting-to-know-you weekends. No pressure, no rush."

"I think I already experienced your idea of 'no pressure.'"

"But as you noted, you kissed me back." Heartened by the wry tone in her voice, he entreated, "I improve over wine and with time." To his relief, Genevieve managed a genuine chuckle. Growing serious again, Marshall added, "Genevieve, I'll unpack and set things out, but you have an eye, I can see that. And you have the added benefit of having seen many of the properties in the area and undoubtedly have seen what works and what doesn't." He softened his voice. "I promise to be the gentleman you want me to be until you feel comfortable with taking things to another level."

She was silent for several more seconds and then said, "I *have* to take this call. Let me think about it, okay?"

"Fair enough."

As Marshall disconnected, he wasn't entirely satisfied. He would have liked her to say that she would call him back later, see him tonight, but at least she hadn't turned him down outright. He would have to find the patience to wait for her to give him what she could of herself. Just the thought had him feeling restless and depressed again. But remembering what he'd promised her, he went to attack the nearest stack of boxes.

As soon as Genevieve disconnected from the call that had been holding on her office phone, Avery Pageant pushed open her door and with her usual untimid style draped herself over the nearest of the two chairs facing the cluttered desk. Avery's exotic Eastern scent followed then settled around the brunette like an intoxicating presence signaling anyone without eyes that she wasn't a woman who expected to be overlooked or taken for granted.

"Since when do you close your office door when you aren't with clients?" she asked, glancing at Genevieve over her red reading glasses.

Genevieve didn't stop shuffling through the yellow phone messages their receptionist-secretary Ina Bargas had handed her when she'd entered the building, but she knew it was useless to ignore the question entirely. If anyone was more persistent than her mother, it was this woman, whom fellow agent Raenne Hartley teasingly dubbed "Dragon Lady." "I needed a few minutes before this interrogation commenced. But now that you're here, how are you?"

"Taking some exception to the term *interrogation.* I think we should open a bottle of wine at your place or mine after work—yours, mine hasn't been dusted or vacuumed in ten days—and get in some serious girl talk."

Genevieve dropped the phone messages, only to gesture expansively. "Are you not looking at this disaster? I'll be here making sense of things until at least nine tonight."

"The price of success. Cooperative soul that I am, I volunteer to go get the wine and help you. We can talk in between phone calls and printouts. It'll be the working woman's pajama party."

"I have a better idea—I'll buy you a bottle of wine if you'll go away."

"I actually sold more property than you did this month,

I can buy my own wine. Talk to me, darn it. He's made you all hot and bothered—and that's a good thing."

"I'm not ready, Avery."

"Elaborate, please. You're not ready for a relationship or to talk about what happened at his place?"

Oh, murder, Genevieve thought, did she have every thought mirrored on her face? "I will give you my very next referral regardless of the potential value of the property if you will please change the subject."

Looking a bit impatient, the brunette crossed her legs, her black designer slacks whispering as linen brushed linen. Then she straightened the collar of her red silk shirt. "You may not think four years is long enough to prove that you were devoted to Adam, but from this side of our age difference, I assure you, I'm convinced. I suspect so is every person in this freaking town who is watching you waste your youth."

Aghast at her boldness, particularly since Avery had divorced twice, Genevieve gasped. "Stop it! You have no right to tell me how I should feel or behave. You don't know a thing about it."

"No, I don't. But I have a right to worry about you."

Her sudden tender tone and gentle look had Genevieve shaking her head. "Thank you," she grumbled.

"The truth is I'd like to feel that deeply about someone just once," Avery replied ruefully. "So was that Mr. Hold-On-To-Your-Heart Roark you were talking to on your BlackBerry just now? You just left him and he's *already* calling you? Why couldn't I have been born a honey-eyed blonde?"

"You're perfect just the way you are," Genevieve replied in total honesty. "A little scary at times, but I know there are strong men who aren't intimidated by that."

Avery sucked in her cheeks as she continued her speculation, which added to the sharpness of her high cheekbones and sharper chin. With her ear-length bob, the rinse-enhanced brunette reminded Genevieve of a modern-day Cleopatra, who had also been purported to be no great beauty, but a captivating character nonetheless.

"Trying to shut me up with flattery?"

"Did it work?"

"Almost." Avery tilted her head as she studied her. "You may not want to hear this either, but I do think it's started."

That got Genevieve's attention. "What has?"

"The remoteness that's been like a fog around you all this time. It's lifting. You're less the Ghost of Genevieve Past and more present. Bravo."

Sneaky, conniving woman, Genevieve thought, returning to sorting her files into stacks. But she was determined not to be totally suckered in by Avery. "Thank you...I think."

"Damn it, G.G., don't make me wish your luscious Mr. Roark would have called me instead of you. He's what, closing in on forty?"

"Thirty-eight."

For a moment Avery was nonplussed, then she shrugged. "That's only four years younger than me. He does comes off as older."

"He takes life seriously. In case you haven't noticed, he's had reason to."

"I could redirect his focus. Maybe even teach him a few things."

"I doubt it."

Snickering, Avery rose. "Well done, Sleeping Beauty. Okay, I've had my fun." She floated the paper she'd come in with so that it landed in front of Genevieve covering what she'd been pretending to peruse. "I just wanted you to know I'm dropping the Ferris property. It's overpriced and you'll see by my notes on all of the calls I've received after viewings that prospective buyers concur."

Genevieve winced at the number of negative comments. "Are Mr. and Mrs. Ferris that clueless about the market that they're resisting a price adjustment?"

"Blinded by ego and greed." A veteran in the business, Avery pulled no punches. "Like too many, they feel a smart buyer will recognize all that they're getting for that money."

Genevieve studied the address to refresh her memory. "Okay, but isn't this the house at the end of a dirt road where people have used the woods for dumping?"

"Bingo. Quite an attractive and well-kept property, but out of the city limits. Those woods could have a trailer parked on adjoining land next week and a meth lab operation thereafter. Too much of a risk for a buyer."

"In that case, I'm with you—release them."

"Thanks. Oh, and Raenne is on her way back from her viewing."

Relieved, Genevieve asked, "Did she hint at how it went?"

"The buyers are following her in to fill out a contract."

"Wonderful." Genevieve knew better than to assume

anything before it happened, but she was proud of Raenne and grateful for the good news for the agency. "That one would make a nice 'sold' announcement in our newspaper ad next week."

"I thought you'd want to do that. Some of our rural clients are getting so depressed with the slow market." Avery retrieved her printout from Genevieve's desk. "I'll make this call before I head out to meet my afternoon appointment."

"Good luck with them. I know they're wearing you out, too."

"It hasn't been my easiest account, but I have a good feeling about this house I'm showing them today."

No sooner did Avery leave then Genevieve's Black-Berry started playing Beethoven's infamous Fifth. That immediately informed her that the caller was her mother. "Mother, unless Bart has run off with Dorothy," she said referring to her mother's full-time housekeeper, "I don't have time for this."

Sydney Sawyer clucked in exasperation. "That's not remotely amusing, Gigi, and why is it that you can eke out an hour here and five there for everyone but *me?*"

Her earlier suspicions about being watched confirmed, Genevieve said wryly, "Could be because you're a notorious busybody and you're not interested in attention from me, you only want to fish for more information about Marshall Roark."

"For your information," her mother replied with maximum hauteur, "I was merely going to ask if he was officially settled in and would be staying around for a while? I'd like Dorothy to bring over a casserole and pie.

He must be thinking we're all barbarians what with our lack of neighborly concern."

"Mother, are you about to write a flashback scene? Because you're sounding dangerously close to a conniving Scarlett in *Gone with the Wind*."

"Obviously, all of this extra responsibility is taking a toll on your poor nerves," Sydney replied.

Genevieve was minimally apologetic. "That and constant interruptions since I've returned to the office. Just leave the man alone. The movers have barely left and he's been through enough for a few days. And don't even think of casting him in one of your stories. That's not an empty threat. I've already warned him about you."

"You what?" Recovering, Sidney summoned regal disdain. "Even if I wanted to, I couldn't possibly. I'm booked three years out. By then I may be too old to do more than watch Bart fondle his cigar collection."

"Let him fondle. When his doctor warned him that his heart couldn't take many more smokes, it was a blow to his ego." Her mother's self-pitying forecasting had Genevieve massaging her brow. "At any rate, in three years, you'll still be too young to collect social security."

"Finally, a compliment from my own flesh and blood. Now why on earth did you stay over at his house for so long?"

"I reminded you the other day. I'd agreed to supervise the movers."

"I mean *after* they left."

Had she used a stopwatch, for pity's sake? "Marshall asked for decorating input." Genevieve figured she might as well get that out there; otherwise she would be accused of hiding something if she was spotted back there again—not that she was convinced that would be a good idea.

Her mother's opinion was immediately clear.

"You can't be serious? He can afford the best in the business. You're a real estate broker, not Martha Stewart."

"And, unlike Martha, obviously a one-dimensional human being."

"Oh, don't be so thin-skinned, dear," Sydney replied. "You know I adore what you've done with your house— and the input you gave me on mine for that matter—but am I wrong?"

"No, mother. However, professionals need and want to use their clients' names for publicity. Could you conceive that Marshall doesn't want it advertised and blabbed everywhere about where he's living and what he's spending?"

"He has to meet new people at some point. He is planning to stay, isn't he?"

Her mother never lingered on a subject that didn't feel immediately profitable to her. "Mother, I have to return no less than seven phone calls. Was there something specific that you needed?"

"Just let me know when you plan another trip over there," Sydney replied. "I'll help you. This way we'll get introductions out of the way, and I can deliver the food, too."

"I haven't committed myself, but if I do I'll think about it," Genevieve replied and disconnected. Introducing Sydney to Marshall? It would, she thought, be less painful to step in front of a runaway semi.

* * *

Genevieve didn't call her mother back that day, or the next. She didn't call Marshall, either. But on Saturday evening, once the rest of the office had long gone home and it was almost dark, she knew to delay things any longer would be unfair as well as rude, and she rang him.

"I've been worried about you," he began, probably thanks to caller ID.

"I'm sorry. It's been—"

"I can imagine."

Genevieve hesitated, wondering if he was being sympathetic or suspecting that she was handing him a line and wanted her to move on to her reason for finally deigning to call. "Is it too late for me to stop by?" she asked.

"Come on over."

Dusk had turned into night by the time she pulled into Marshall's driveway and a quick glance toward her mother's house told her that the upstairs office lights were off. Hopefully, Bart had insisted on going out somewhere. He was twice the social butterfly that her mother was and the couple had an agreement that Sydney not work on weekends.

Marshall stood in the open doorway as she came up the sidewalk. In the glow of the dangling light fixture, she could see that his lips were curved in welcome, but his gaze was definitely gauging her mood and body language. This was the last real summer weekend before the Labor Day weekend and she'd had two closings, a showing and a contract to process today. She didn't have to pretend to be tired, but she had apparently held up well enough.

As she entered, he leaned over to kiss her cheek and said, "You look wonderful."

She'd worn a favorite white suit because it was her last chance for the season—at least by fashionista standards. "My aching feet disagree."

"Feel free to make yourself comfortable," he said as he closed the door behind her. He gestured to his own bare feet. "As you can see I am."

Wearing a black T-shirt and jeans, he did look ultra-casual, but his understated attire did nothing to mute his physical appeal. It was as though all of the energy in the universe was working in tandem to force her to stay aware of that.

"The problem is that if I took off these heels, I might never get them on again." Although that was the truth, it was only half of it. "I can't stay," she added quietly.

"Somehow I knew you would say something like that. At least join me in a glass of wine," Marshall replied. "I'd just finished unpacking the last box and showered when you called. I have muscles demanding relief."

She'd noticed that his hair was still somewhat damp. Thinking a drink would also help her say what she had to say, she accepted. As she followed him, she noted the only lights on were in the kitchen, and those were the accent ones above the cabinets. It made their environment more intimate, yet provided enough illumination for him to work.

"Did you really finished unpacking?" she asked, eyeing the bare counters that she'd left stacked two and three boxes high. Now there was only a toaster, a coffeemaker and a paper towel stand. "Everything?"

"Yes. Well, except for the one bedroom." Marshall drew a bottle of wine from the refrigerator and took two fat goblets from the buffet. "I'll call a charity and donate her clothes—unless you know of someone who could use them around here?"

"I do. There's a church-operated store in town that would welcome the donation. I'll get you the number."

"Thanks." With minimal physical effort, he uncorked the wine.

His unwillingness to speak Cynthia's name brought her reticence about Adam back to mind. "I didn't follow my own advice with Adam's things," she blurted out. "I brought them down to a charity in Tyler. I was afraid I'd be driving down the street here one day and see his favorite shirt or jacket."

"I won't have that problem," he said, pouring the first drops of wine into his glass, then filling hers one-third full. "As you saw for yourself, Cyn never veered from the same style thing that she'd worn through college—jeans, Dockers, T-shirts and sweatshirts. Her things will blend in fine here."

Genevieve nodded. "I remember her saying that she'd been a tomboy and athletic. I suppose comfort was her chief motivation later."

"That and doing her best to discourage any sexual interest I might have in her."

"Oh, Marshall." There didn't seem to be anything she could say that wasn't going to trigger pain, and maybe even bitterness in him. That was never her intention.

"Sorry." He held out her glass to her. "I did understand, even though I didn't always handle things well."

"I could see you did—and cared. And from what I could tell, you were very attentive and gentle with her." Genevieve set her keys on the counter and accepted the goblet. She'd left her purse in the car to give him another sign that she was serious about not staying but a few minutes. "Okay, subject change—are you going to give me a tour? It sounds like you really pushed it."

"Wait until you see." Although he touched his glass to hers, there was a hint of mockery or self-deprecation in his voice. "But first, tell me more about your day. Do you realize how long it's been since I had an intelligent conversation? Of course you do—you were it!"

After an initial sip of her wine, Genevieve was about to point out that she could hear the TV on somewhere and knew he had a satellite dish hooked up, but then again that wasn't a conversation, that was all one-sided. "Well, we gained two new residents today," she told him. "A dentist and a nurse, both from Dallas."

"Are they a couple?"

"No, each has a spouse."

"Having professionals moving in is a good sign."

"It is. Our dentist, Dr. Harvey, is retiring and selling his practice to a young doctor. Tim Petrie. Unless you keep your Dallas doctor, you'll probably meet him sooner or later. He and his wife are energetic and enjoy canoeing."

"Are they here on the lake?"

"Interestingly, no. In town about three blocks from his office. They bought a historical home. Mrs. Petrie's other interest is antiques and restorations."

"I remember seeing it. I liked it myself, but three stories wasn't practical for us. So you've saved a local bit of history from further deterioration, as well. That should provide some job satisfaction."

"I liken it to the pebble-skipping-across-calm-water metaphor. The ripples expand and sometimes merge. You get to see lives touching lives here."

"Well put. Unlike in the vast sea of Dallas where a pebble vanishes amid all the other frenetic motion going on," he drawled.

"Okay, you got me. I'm prejudiced." Smiling, Genevieve lifted her glass. It was a lovely cabernet that he'd briefly cooled to perfection. "This is sheer bliss," she said after a second sip.

"It is now."

Those three words cast them back to where they'd been the other day when she'd pulled away from his kiss and her own temptation and fled, stunned and in conflict with the emotions he'd stirred in her. Fighting that new magnetic pull, she gestured toward the dark living room. "Show me what you've accomplished."

"If you insist, although you might want to delay another taste of the wine," he said, maneuvering around her to turn on the ceiling lights.

It took Genevieve only a second to realize what he'd done and burst into laughter before she clapped her free hand over her mouth.

"Aha," she said once she'd recovered. "So this is the other kind of 'unpacked.'"

Everything was piled on every table surface available as though for an estate sale—lamps, accent pieces, books and collectibles. Even the couches and chairs were loaded. Carpets were unrolled, but piled knee-high in the middle of the room. Paintings were lined against the walls and windows like suspects in a police lineup.

His dark blue eyes twinkling, Marshall replied, "I warned you that I didn't know what to do with all of this."

"Well, actually, this isn't as bad as you may have wanted it to look. At least this way you can see what you have to work with." She cast him a skeptical sidelong glance. "But what does the garage area look like—a fire hazard?"

"The Dallas Mavericks could stand shoulder-to-shoulder and you couldn't find them in that paper-and-cardboard mountain."

Genevieve believed it was that bad. The movers had done a good job because much of the Roarks' artwork looked to be pieces with a provenance—or at least limited-number prints. "A recycling truck stops at the city hall the first Saturday of every month. They collect bundled newspapers, magazines and cardboard, bagged paper products," she recited, "plastic bottles and aluminum cans."

"That's probably a smarter plan than buying someone's decrepit barge and creating my own Viking pyre on the lake."

This was her first glimpse of his sense of humor and Genevieve was charmed. "No doubt, Beau Stanton would have been inspired to write a song, and you'd certainly become a hero to the kids around here." She began to navigate her way through the clutter so she could get a closer look at what he had. "You like landscapes. I should have guessed that from your earth tones in the furniture and linens. These are wonderful. The windows bring the outdoors inside, and this artwork will continue that."

"Well, once upon a time I liked to camp and hike, but the more breathing problems Cyn developed, the less opportunity there was for that."

"I suspect that the businesses must have kept you busier and busier, too," Genevieve said. She would hate it if he let himself see Cynthia as the cause for everything he'd had to give up. But as soon as she met his gaze, she knew he was onto her.

"There was that," he said. "It was right when we knew her full diagnosis that I got the buyout offer and recognized it as the opportunity to use what time was left to take life slower."

His shrug suggested those good intentions were too late, and when he lifted his glass, he drank the wine as though it was scotch.

Genevieve appreciated his forthrightness, but not that it was coming at such a price, and she did her best to once again focus on the art. "I would put those two black-and-white photos of the mist-drenched forest in your bathroom," she said, pointing to the framed pieces a few feet away. "With the silvery-green wallpaper in there and your brown-and-green towels, they'll add the perfect ambiance, especially after a shower when the room is foggy."

He nodded, his introverted expression indicating he was picturing her suggestion. Then, reaching over to pick them up in one hand, he said, "Let's go see if that looks as perfect as it sounds."

His excitement was as intoxicating as the wine and she followed, admitting to herself that she was glad she'd accepted the wine and didn't just blurt out what she'd come to say and run away like a coward. She liked him, was drawn to him, and it wasn't his fault that she was just not ready, and might never be.

It turned out that the TV she'd heard was playing in his office. As they passed there, Marshall leaned in to key the remote and shut it off. That made things ultra-quiet as they entered the master suite.

"Sorry about the noise," he said. "It must strike you as odd that a person who enjoyed the solitude and quiet of the outdoors would have the TV all but blaring."

"Not at all. I did the same thing in the beginning. Only for me it was airhead comedies that require no thinking. I couldn't risk anything that would make me cry for fear of never stopping."

"Of course. The last thing you needed was the latest body count from overseas."

As they entered the master bedroom, he flipped on a few lights, then turned left into his vanity area. Only a hint of dampness and warmth remained from his shower, and she could see that he'd left the room immaculate, but her imagination went into overdrive anyway and she pictured him emerging from the shower stall.

The click of Marshall's glass on the brown marble counter jerked her back to reality, and she watched, feeling a little dazed, as he held up the framed photos above the brass towel rack and against the green-striped wallpaper.

"Is this what you mean?"

Genevieve looked from the photos over her shoulder at the mirror and saw her hunch was on target. The photos would be beautifully reflected in the vanity mirror, as well. "Perfect. Don't you think so?"

"At the risk of sounding egotistical, yeah. When I first framed them, I thought at best they could fill a dark hallway somewhere or be donated to a garage sale. They've spent most of their life in a closet. Cyn thought black-and-white photos were depressing."

As he stood back and crossed his arms over his chest as though reminiscing, Genevieve understood and gasped. "*You're* the photographer."

"It's been years since I picked up a camera. This is the Cascades in Washington just after I graduated from high school."

"You were a teenager when you took these? They're so mature. You found the strength as well as the isolation of nature. That takes some special sensitivity, I would think."

"Whatever it is, it's long lost or buried." He set the frames onto the carpet and leaned them against the wall. "Care to try another hunch?"

"Don't you want to hang these?"

"I can do that tomorrow when you're not here. I don't want to waste my muse's time. Especially when she's nervous about being around me."

Almost relieved that the issue was finally out in the open, Genevieve said, "I would happily help you, Marshall, but we both know that's not all you want."

He brushed her hair back over one shoulder, only to reclaim one strand to wrap around his finger. "You did admit that you kissed me back."

"After which I began to feel as though I'd been cheating."

"Unless you're keeping company with a ghost, you can't cheat on what no longer exists."

Genevieve felt caught in a web, trapped by his charisma, while at the same time being pulled away into the vacuum that was her fading memory. She moved her goblet to hold it with both hands as though any barrier was better than none. "The fact remains that I still feel married."

"Since you didn't when I was kissing you the other day, I think the solution is to kiss you more."

Chapter Three

Marshall hadn't intended for things to come to this when he'd first grabbed up the photos and led Genevieve back here to the master suite. He was too grateful to have her here giving him input with what to do with everything to risk upsetting or offending her. At the same time, he was discovering that he couldn't be near her without needing to touch her, and when she'd praised his work, he felt as if he'd seen his first glimpse of sunshine after an endless darkness. Someone else might be strong enough to resist responding to that, but he was far too human. Too hungry.

As he lowered his head, she whispered, "Marshall, please don't."

"Stop thinking for once. Just for one minute…feel… me."

His kiss was as tender and coaxing as his words, his lips brushing over hers before skimming over to her cheek and chin, then back to her mouth. With slightly more pressure, he parted her lips and sought entry with his tongue. Genevieve tried to stop him again by touching her fingers to his mouth, but he only took hold of her hand and kissed each fingertip. All the while his gaze held hers. He could see as well as feel and hear his growing effect on her—the way her eyes dilated and her breath grew shallow, and the way her glass bumped against his chest as she began to lose herself in what was happening between them. Taking the crystal from her, he blindly reached behind him to set it on the counter next to his, then he wrapped both arms around her and drew her completely against him.

"*Genevieve*. I could say your name all night. I want to." She felt unbelievable fitted against him—and not just because it had been a long time for him. The taste of her went straight to his head. With her to intoxicate him, his sore muscles didn't need wine. But she wasn't totally willing to be swept away. Although she let her eyelids drift closed, seduced by his caresses, her fingers sought and gripped at his shirt.

"Kiss me back," he coaxed. "Let go and wrap your arms around me. Hold me like I'm holding you. Need me like this."

He'd never been so open with a woman. Comfortable, yes, but naked with his vulnerability to another soul, never. That honesty must have reached her because she did release his shirt and she slowly slid her arms over his shoulders to caress his neck and sink her fingers into his hair just as her tongue began answering his bolder strokes.

God, yes, he thought, growing hot and hard. He could

feel her breasts grow taut and he wanted to see her, taste her. When he trailed his fingers down her sides to caress the subtle curves, she whimpered into his mouth, and brought his hand back to fully cover her. He stroked her with his thumb and then bent to cover her with his mouth.

She gasped and trembled as though struck by lightning and held on tighter. Marshall could feel the tremors of his own excitement and need, too.

Guided by touch alone, he unbuttoned her jacket and spread the silk to stroke his hands over her lacy bra and the creamy perfection he'd exposed. "You're so beautiful." He feathered kisses all over her satin-smooth skin. "Beautiful," he said again as he unclasped the front fastener. Then she was bared to him and he worshipped her with his hands and mouth. When he wasn't suckling and enticing one breast, he was cupping the other and keeping her taut with his thumb.

Things slipped a little more out of control after that. It felt as though they'd already drunk the entire bottle of wine and Genevieve even reached out blindly to steady herself and accidentally hit the light switch, casting the room into darkness.

As Marshall returned to feast on her mouth, he cupped her hips and rocked himself against her. At the same time, she bunched up his shirt so that their bodies from the waist up were flesh to flesh.

"I have to..." he rasped, bunching up her narrow skirt. "We have to."

Her hair veiled her face as she pressed her head to his shoulder and rubbed herself against him. His chest hairs teasing her nipples all but drove her wild, and she began fumbling with the top button of his jeans. The barrier of that little bit of lace between her legs nearly had him shredding them. Once he'd stripped her, he finished opening his jeans and lifted her over him.

"Genevieve," he rasped in half apology, half plea.

"Please," she whispered.

He tried to be careful; she was so tight, but she was also wet and hot, and wrapping her legs around him. He lost his head. Locking his mouth to hers, he pressed her harder against the wall and drove into her repeatedly, devouring her moans and, after two more thrusts, her cry of ecstasy. The next thrust brought his own.

As the all-consuming wave of passion receded, their hearts continued to pound as one. Marshall buried his face in Genevieve's hair as he fought to catch his breath. He didn't want reality to intrude, didn't know what he would do if he looked into her eyes and saw regret. Pressing an openmouthed kiss against the curve between her neck and shoulder, he felt himself pulsate inside her as his appetite stirred anew. "Give me a few more seconds and I'll do this properly on, if not in, the bed," he said, thinking he hadn't recovered this quickly since he was eighteen.

The promise was barely spoken when the front doorbell rang.

"What the hell...?" he began.

"Murder," Genevieve moaned. Reality came more quickly to her—like an icy slap. "Let me down." Even as she unwrapped her legs, Marshall protested.

"Let's ignore it."

How could they? "My car is in your driveway, and I'll

bet you that's my mother out there." There wasn't time to explain how she knew. Once he knew Sydney Sawyer, he would understand. "Go! I'll follow as soon as I can."

He went, making himself presentable along the way. By the time Genevieve turned on the lights again, she heard the water running in the next bathroom, which told her that he'd paused to freshen up himself.

She quickly fastened her bra and jacket, and stepped back into her panties. Her mind was racing like a Grand Prix driver thinking of how she could explain to her mother being back in Marshall Roark's bedroom, but then she caught sight of herself in the vanity mirror.

She gasped in horror. Her white suit had an *O* around her left breast. She might be able to get out the wine with a little work, but not now. Not without leaving a wet mark that would be another dead giveaway to her mother, whose vision even in low lighting—*please, Marshall, don't flip on every freaking switch in the place*—was second only to an X-ray machine.

Upon hearing a painfully familiar soprano voice, Genevieve uttered an expletive under her breath. Yes, that was definitely her mother.

Glancing back at her reflecting, she winced. "Poor suit," she murmured, knowing what she had to do. Taking up her glass, she doused the front of her jacket with most of the remaining wine.

The effects were as awful as she expected they would be, but at least the incriminating stain was hidden. Quickly wetting the washrag on the counter, she went to join Marshall and his untimely visitor, or more likely visitors, since wherever Sydney was at this hour, Bart couldn't be far behind. All the while she dabbed at and fussed with the stain.

"I'm sorry, Marshall," she said, emerging from the hallway. She pretended to be oblivious to what else might be going on as she entered the living room. "I think your carpet is safe, but—" she timed her glance up, so she could pretend surprise at seeing her mother and Bart "—oh. What are you two doing here?"

They looked as if they were back from an upscale bowling tournament, both dressed in matching gold designer sweat suits. Of course, her mother wore at least a pound of gold jewelry that sparkled and jangled with her every move. Her strawberry-blond helmet hair was almost as bright.

"Evening, sweetheart," Bart replied, rubbing his index finger along his nose and keeping his gaze on the hardwood floor. "Sorry for the interruption, but you know your mother."

After elbowing her dashing silver-haired husband in his ribs, Sydney arched a finely plucked eyebrow at her. "What on earth have you done to that lovely suit, dear?"

"Don't worry about the carpet," Marshall said before Genevieve could answer. "It's my fault. After all, I bumped you."

She went weak with relief that he caught on so quickly. "Only because I was crowding you to see where you meant to hang those photos." Was that too much explaining? By her writer-mother's speculative expression, she was sure it was, but it was too late. Shrugging, she said to them, "Marshall had unfinished packing tonight and asked if I had some time to help him place some pictures."

Sydney peered around the dimly lit room at the bare walls. "Starting in the bedrooms?"

Ignoring her, Genevieve gestured with the washrag. "Excuse me, have you all already handled introductions?"

"As awkwardly as nosy neighbors can," Bart drawled.

"Oh, Bart, really," Sydney muttered. "Does a mother not have a right to worry about her only child?" To Genevieve she said, "When we were heading to Polly and Sam's to play forty-two, we saw you still working at the office. And here we are on the way home and you're still at it."

Obviously, that was Marshall's cue and he offered a brief, formal bow. "I did and do feel guilty for adding to her workload, Mrs. Sawyer."

"Conway," Bart said on a sigh. "Sawyer is just her stage name."

As Bart won another withering look from his wife, Genevieve decided her mother had humiliated her enough.

"Don't play to that performance," Genevieve told Marshall. "Bart got it right." She plucked at the clammy and stained material. "You know what? This suit feels equally uncomfortable. I'm going to get my keys and get home. Maybe I can still save this outfit if I start soaking it soon enough."

Wholly unruffled, Sydney said, "Come to the house, darling. You know there's never been a stain that could resist my ministrations, and I'm sure you can find something in my closet since we wear the same size in most things."

"Except in muzzle," Bart offered to Marshall.

Equally embarrassed at her mother's unveiled compliment to herself, Genevieve sent him a grateful smile before telling her mother, "Thanks, but this is Bart's night for your undivided attention, isn't it, St. Bart?"

"Bless you, my child. Once a week I know what it's like to go to sleep with my wife beside me," he explained to Marshall. "Otherwise it takes a power outage to tear the woman from that damned computer."

As Sydney began, "Now, Bart, really..." Genevieve hurried to the kitchen, where she dropped the washrag in the sink and grabbed her keys. Back in the entryway, she touched Marshall's arm, but only made fleeting eye contact. "I hope the suggestions helped. Mother, Bart, 'night." She added a kiss to her stepfather's cheek as she passed.

Hurrying to her vehicle, she knew this was not over—neither for her mother nor Marshall. Regarding her mother, Genevieve would have plenty to say herself, so the woman who had given birth to her had better rethink calling tonight. As for Marshall...what had she done?

Once in her SUV, she could barely get her key into the ignition, her hands were shaking so much. Of all the humiliating experiences, she thought—and not just because of her mother and Bart's inopportune arrival. What had possessed her to let things go that far with Marshall?

That was the point—he'd possessed her.

For the entire drive home, she stressed. She'd let him take her as if she was the town tramp. How could she ever look him in the eyes again without turning as red as if she was sun-scorched?

By the time she pulled into her driveway, her Black-Berry was going berserk. Her mother and Marshall were taking turns jamming up her connection. She was no-where near ready to deal with either of them. She needed a shower. She was radiating Marshall's scent and the insane thing was that it was arousing her again!

Once parked in her garage, she collected her things and hurried inside. With the BlackBerry continuing to go strong, she felt hunted, so she turned it off.

Before she could strip and step into the shower, her house phone began to ring. Of course, Marshall had this number, too. She always gave her best and favorite clients all three numbers. For the first time, she regretted that.

No, you don't, you're just scared of yourself more than him.

True. Stepping under the hot spray, she couldn't touch her own body without trembling from the reminder of his touch, of how it felt to have him inside her. Turning the spray to its sharpest, she welcomed the liquid pum-meling willing it to beat her numb.

So wrong…so wrong.

Her landline was ringing again when she turned off the water and wrapped herself in her white terry-cloth robe and her dripping hair in a towel. Knowing she would have him on her doorstep if she didn't answer, Genevieve crossed the bedroom to reach for the phone beside the bed.

She confirmed the number on the phone's screen, and her first words were hardly an apology. "I needed to shower."

"I'd hoped that's what you were doing, but considering the hour and you living alone—I was worried."

His tone was gruff as though he'd been verbally berating himself since she left, but his concern was sweet. Yet that just created all the more conflict for her. "That's— Thank you."

"How are you, Genevieve?"

When he lowered his voice to that deep decibel, Genevieve remembered when he'd uttered, "Need me." She had to bite back a moan because she felt it at her most sensitive parts. "Oh, that's not a good question to ask at the moment. How long did Mother and Bart stay?"

"About two minutes at the most. He pretty much tugged her out the door telling her that he would never let her drive home again. I like him."

"So do I. But, Marshall, this won't stop now. She senses something and she's been ringing whatever number you're not using since you started calling. I had to turn off my BlackBerry."

"I guessed as much when I would get a busy signal. About that wine stain—I hated that you felt the need to take blame for the carpet when you knew it was perfectly fine. And while staining your dress was brilliant—"

"Actually, I didn't think about the carpet. I'm sorry. All I knew was walking out of your bedroom with your mouth imprint flagrantly on my chest would have been far worse."

"My...?" Groaning, he said, "Genevieve...I didn't think."

"Neither of us were doing much of that."

"I'm definitely replacing that lovely suit."

"That's the least of my worries."

A frown entered his voice. "Why are you worried? No, first go back to my first question—how are you? Did I hurt you?"

"*No.* Marshall, what I'm feeling isn't about you." *Well, not entirely anyway.*

"Thanks."

Genevieve winced at his dejection. "That's not what I meant. You were wonderful."

He drew a long, relieved breath. "I so wanted to take you to my bed and show you that I'm not without finesse."

"I know what you are, what you're capable of. If I didn't, what happened couldn't have happened in the first place."

"Let me come over. This isn't a conversation that should happen over the phone. Besides, I'm aching to be with you again."

As her gaze fell on a picture of Adam on the night-stand, her heart wrenched. "Stop! I mean...Marshall, you can't. I have neighbors, too." Sweet older ones who had been asleep for hours, but didn't need to see a strange man leaving her driveway in the wee hours of the morning as they rose like all old people did to pace for insomnia or medical issues, often peering outside to make sure all was well on their quiet cul-de-sac.

"You're killing me, Genevieve."

She turned her back to the photo and sat down on the edge of the bed. "I'm not feeling too well myself."

"I can hear that, and my hunch is that you're going to try to freeze me out now because you're convincing yourself that what we shared was a mistake."

"It was."

"Don't say that, darling."

"Marshall…the other reason you can't come over is because I'm not on birth control." She heard him draw a sharp breath and continued quickly, "Don't worry, I'm sure it's all right, but that tells you that I meant it when I said that I still felt married. There hasn't been anyone else."

"I should have known. You're not the kind of woman to indulge in casual sex. Then I should have known when it wasn't easy for you to take me."

Genevieve had to press her thighs together and bend at the waist to keep her body from being seduced all over again by his voice and words. "Please…stop."

"All I can do is apologize again, sweetheart. I wasn't prepared, either, even if this had been premeditated." He laughed briefly. "I'm that out of practice."

That was something she should cherish, but it only left her with a stark realization. "Then I guess it's not entirely a bad thing that my mother and Bart dropped by. I think one try at Russian roulette is enough for two misfit singles like us, don't you?"

"What I think is that we really need to talk, and not over the phone. Is the office open tomorrow?"

"No, we try to stay closed Sundays—and I sing in the church choir," she added, a strong hint in case he had some idea about breakfast or brunch.

"I would have guessed you could sing. Your speaking voice is melodious. Soprano?"

"Yes," she said, a little confused by the way he was veering off the point.

"Second?"

"First."

"What color robe?"

The man was definitely keeping her off balance. "Peppermint stripes," she replied, feeling a bit rebellious. "What are you doing?"

"Learning about you. I may have gotten some critical things out of sequence, but I'm a quick study. What color?"

"Gold."

His murmur spoke of satisfaction. "That's a nice image. With your hair and eyes, you must look like an angel. Can I take you to lunch afterward?"

Speaking of voices, his was returning to that tender seductive tone that could get under her defenses way too easily. "Thank you, and that's a tempting offer, but I really better get over to Mother's and remind her of some boundaries she's not respecting."

"She's undeniably a character, but it's easy to see why Bart puts up with her and keeps that twinkle in his eyes. She's quite an attractive woman. You hit a payload in the gene department."

"She would love hearing that—and thank you yet again. You know, if I don't get this wet hair blow-dried, I'm going to have to get back in the shower and rinse it again. It has a mind of its own."

"I'd like to see your wild woman look—it sounds enticing. I'm going to put it at the top of my wish list."

"Marshall…"

"I know, I know, but if I let you hang up, you'll have time to think and I can't see how that will work in my favor. At least consider stopping by after you're done at your mother's tomorrow? You saw the condition of this place. Doesn't that trigger any sympathy for my predicament?"

"None." But she couldn't stop a smile from entering her voice. "Let me sleep on it, okay?"

"And how are you going to be able to do that? I won't."

"I'm hanging up now," she said softly. "Goodnight."

After drying her hair, she tried to catch up on e-mails and paperwork, but she also paced around the house. She'd bought the modest white-brick home located on a maple-lined street near the library and city hall, not long after she'd gotten into real estate and started to have regular success. Adam had never been in this house. She'd bought it with her first year's earnings when she began at another agency. But his photographs were scattered around the house, and she spoke to them—or sighed at them—regularly. Tonight, she could barely bring herself to acknowledge they were there.

Her mother was one issue—a headache that she'd been dealing with all of her life. This situation with Marshall was an even bigger problem for her. It wasn't natural to feel guilt about what had happened tonight. She was single and free to date. So was Marshall. In her mind, she'd betrayed no law of man or God. And yet Adam still owned her heart. With that reality, how could she have let another man make love to her?

Call it what it was—sex. That's all.

She shivered, disliking the coldness of the term and wrapped her arms tighter around herself despite the warm robe. It wasn't fair to her or Marshall. Maybe she couldn't call it love, but try as she might, she couldn't deny that she had feelings for him, and he apparently did for her.

It was grief and loneliness that had brought them to this and that wasn't anything to be ashamed about. So why couldn't she just accept that she was transitioning?

Maybe because that would mean letting go of all she had left of Adam—her sorrow. Marshall didn't seem to be having this problem. He was flirting and ready to openly pursue her.

"Men are definitely different," she said to the empty room.

At church the next day, she half expected to see Marshall in the congregation, but then he never asked what church she belonged to and there were several in town and over a hundred in their county. Her mother and Bart were present, though, and her mother was looking happy and approving since Genevieve finally had called her last night and invited herself to lunch.

After services, she was a half hour behind them since she had to put up her robe and lingered to catch up with friends. When she let herself into the house, she almost stopped in her tracks to see Bart handing Marshall a scotch and water, while her mother, holding a glass of cabernet, stood by, beaming even more than she had in church.

"Here she is," Sydney all but sang. "Pour her a glass of wine, Bart. Gigi, isn't it wonderful that I could talk Marshall into making it a foursome for lunch?"

Closing the door gave her a chance to quell the return of frustration with her mother's underhanded ways, as well to ride out that first startling skip in her pulse at seeing Marshall. And drat the man, he was also looking at her as though reliving every second of last night despite his fixed smile. She dropped her keys into the sage-green clutch bag that matched her linen sheath and heels and placed it on the entryway table.

"Wonderful," she said dryly. Not only had her mother known inviting him would save her from a scolding, but she could watch the two of them interact like a lab technician observing specimens through a microscope.

She crossed the Italian marble floor of the grand, circular foyer with its sweeping staircase, and stepped onto the plush ivory rug to join them. "I didn't see the Mercedes," she said to Marshall. "Don't tell me Mother just rang your doorbell again and bribed or blackmailed you to make you come?"

"I walked actually." With a nod to Sydney, he said, "Your mother kindly invited me early this morning before she and Bart left for services. How was choir?"

"Oh, her clarion voice rises above everyone's," Sydney gushed. "You should have studied, Gigi. You'd be an international içon by now doing specials with Michael Bublé and Josh Groban."

"One performer in the family is enough," Genevieve replied. As Bart handed her the goblet with two cocktail napkins, she caught his thumbs-up signal and leaned over to kiss his cheek. "Thank you, St. Bart."

"It's those who love her best, who are asked to suffer the most," he opined.

"I'm an embarrassment to my family," Sydney explained to Marshall. But she hardly looked worried about that.

"Nonsense, love," Bart said, slipping his arm around her waist. "Modesty simply compels us to make you put up your coloring crayons now and again."

Marshall said, "Genevieve has spoken of you with admiration and respect."

Genevieve raised her glass to her mother in a "See there?" salute.

"My daughter doesn't care for what I write," Sydney replied. "What she respects is that I sell lots of books." She preened for Marshall. "I understand your dear late wife was a reader of my work. I'm so sorry that I never got to meet her."

"Mother," Genevieve said quietly, "I'm one observation away from losing my appetite." She felt terrible for Marshall.

His poise intact, he replied, "It's all right." To Sydney he said, "That would have been a thrill for her. You gave her many hours of comfort and pleasure."

"How is it going with the hangings?" Genevieve also gave her mother a look that begged her to move on to a different subject. "Did you accomplish anything else?"

"Well, the ones we thought should be situated in the bathroom are up and they look made for the spot. Following your idea, I think I figured out a good place for four more. You'll have to tell me if I'm on the right track."

"Bart, darling, come help me in the kitchen and let the young people chat," Sydney said. "Genevieve, feel free to show Marshall around the house. We'll check with Dorothy to see how long before lunch is ready."

"Should I talk in her left ear and you in her right?" Bart asked all sweetness. "You always get the good ear."

"Oh, you." Sydney tugged on the sleeve of his sports jacket and led him away.

Once they were alone, Marshall stepped closer to Genevieve. "How's the stain?"

He was no better than wicked Bart, she thought as his gaze slid over her left breast. "A lost cause, I'm afraid—and, no, I'm not taking you up on the offer of a replacement."

"Why not? You wouldn't have had to go to dire straits if I hadn't done what I did."

"Then acknowledging a lesson learned is more than enough reimbursement."

Marshall's gaze turned tender. "You're nothing like the cool professional you exhibit on the job, yet that makes you all the more complicated and intriguing. Quite a bit gets under your skin, and your heart has critical scar tissue. You're a caretaker and nurturer, which is why no matter how frustrating your mother gets, you can't turn your back on her indefinitely. You're a genuine human being, there's nothing shallow about you. And you quite take my breath away."

"Come take the two-dollar tour of the place," she said abruptly, changing the subject and pivoting to lead him back to the foyer. "It really is a gorgeous house."

"Don't be afraid of me," he said, following her. "I'd let them take a limb before I'd knowingly hurt you."

"Sydney actually had this staircase designed from the one in *Gone with the Wind*."

"You look like a mouthwatering scoop of lime sorbet," he murmured, catching up with her. "Cool and delectable."

"If you insist on behaving the way you are, my mother is going to know what's going on before we're finished with the first course."

"I like this subject," he said, swirling the ice in his glass like a New Year's Eve noisemaker. But the instant he saw her stiffen, he added with all seriousness, "Wouldn't it be a relief not to have to pretend?"

"This marble was rescued from a crumbling palazzo in Florence," she said, gesturing to the glistening white and black flooring. "The chandelier was originally a gift to the mistress of a famous Hollywood movie mogul."

"Obviously you don't agree."

"I've gotten as far as to accept that we got carried away," she told him. "To ask for anything else would be too soon."

"What does that mean exactly?" Marshall reached out and swept a strand of her hair back over her shoulder, only to trail his index finger down her bare arm. When she shivered and tried to turn away from him, he stopped her by grasping that arm. "Am I supposed to wait until you tear pages off a hypothetical calendar and gauge I-don't-know-whose perceptions of when it isn't or is appropriate for us to be with each other?"

"We barely escaped what could have been a highly embarrassing and life-complicating predicament," she replied, unable to keep the entreaty from her voice. "Fine. So you're proving that you can touch me and make me respond to you. All that does is leave me with no choice but to keep my distance."

Marshall shook his head. "I'll agree to anything you want short of agreeing not to see you."

Chapter Four

"I think we have a deal."

Genevieve beamed with satisfaction as her clients Glenn and Maureen Bigelow voiced their approval and reached for the pens she'd set on their breakfast-nook table of their home. She had just presented them with an offer on their house for their asking price—unusual in the current market. But location, structure and timing had all played a strong role in the buyers' decision-making—as did the Bigelows' willingness to leave behind a few rooms of furnishings for the young couple recently married and in need of everything.

"Great," she said. "As you can see, I've marked the various paragraphs where I'll need you both to initial and at the end your full, legal signatures."

This house on the east side of Lake Starling was considerably smaller than where her mother and Marshall lived, and about one-third of the price, but it was still a handsome property with wonderful landscaping and boat ramp access to the water. She had met and liked the buyers—Raenne's clients. And this meant more professional people were coming to town—an avionics engineer who was being hired to man the first machine shop at the local airport, and his state police officer wife being transferred up from the San Antonio area.

While the Bigelows went to work, Genevieve picked up her BlackBerry and checked her messages. It was almost four in the afternoon and she was running a good hour behind, which wasn't unusual or problematic for another client, but she hadn't yet eaten except for a donut hole this morning that Ina had popped into her mouth when she'd handed her a coffee to go. No surprise that she was starting to feel shaky and weak. Then again it could be something else. Marshall wanted to take her to dinner in gratitude for what she'd helped him with so far in decorating his house, and she supposed she couldn't get into too much trouble with him if they were in public. But she was worried that she was catching someone's bug. The flu season had, of course, begun weeks ago and she'd gotten her flu shot, but she was fairly certain this wasn't that.

Once the Bigelows pushed the forms back across the table, Glenn—a retired electrician—asked her, "So if all goes well, this October 30th closing date looks good?"

"Raenne tells me your buyers are pre-approved for their mortgage and were renting while trying to find something up here, so there's no second house to wait on selling. You should be settled into your new home in New Mexico in time to entertain for Thanksgiving. Sound good?"

"We're so grateful, Genevieve," retired schoolteacher Maureen said as they all stood. "I can't believe how easy you made this for us."

"You had the desirable property, and made things easy for me," she assured them.

She warned off Maureen at the door when the older woman wanted to hug her, and told them she had to settle for handshakes, provided they wash their hands right after she left. Promising that she would be in touch shortly to confirm matters, she hurried to her car. She was afraid that they would notice she was increasingly nauseous and ready to collapse.

At the office, she went straight for the small pantry next to the fridge to see what was available in the form of a quick sugar surge to get her to dinner. But another wave of nausea had her leaning against the doorjamb and holding one hand over her mouth and her arm around her middle.

Raenne emerged from her office with her empty mug to wash and put up. "Hey, there you are. Did everything go— Whoa. Gen!"

Marshall was entering the quaint cottage that was Gale Realty when he heard a woman cry out. Seeing Ina's reaction as she jumped out of her chair at the front desk, and recognizing that "Gen" probably meant "Genevieve," he raced after the receptionist to the kitchen area. There he found what he feared—Genevieve on the linoleum floor and Raenne kneeling beside her smoothing her hair off her face.

"What's happened?" he demanded, immediately dropping beside her.

"She just sank to the floor," Raenne told him. "Gen, can you hear me?"

Genevieve brushed away the other blonde's hand. "Yes. Please stop fussing."

"Stay put for a second." Marshall signaled Raenne out of the way and took the pulse of the woman who more than ever had become his chief preoccupation since that brief interlude they'd shared in his house three weeks ago. "Do you hurt anywhere?"

"I'd say my pride, but that's a given."

"Your skin is the color of egg mixed with ashes," he told her. "Do you need to get to the bathroom to be sick?"

"Not at the moment. It's passed, I think." Taking a deep breath, Genevieve's frustration surfaced. "Blast it, I'm too busy to get that bug that's knocking everyone on their backsides. If you don't want to catch it, you'd better back up."

Marshall wasn't put off by the warning. "I haven't had a cold in four years and I've never had the flu. You can't scare me."

"Can I videotape you and play it for my supposedly better half?" Raenne asked in all seriousness. "My husband hears me sneeze and he runs for fear that I'll make him too sick to fish at his next bass tournament. Genevieve, let him help you, hon. You really do look as though you've been smelling dead chickens all day."

"And she's being diplomatic," Ina piped in, still clutching her throat.

"Raenne, so help me—" Genevieve shuddered and clapped her hand over her mouth.

It took no effort at all to get her up, but Marshall noted

how modesty became Genevieve's priority over her nausea as she quickly shoved her navy-blue pencil skirt down over her thighs. He caught her self-conscious glance at him and would have smiled at her obvious memory of the last time he saw those lithesome limbs, but sensing she was ultrawobbly—and her strappy, blue-leather heels wouldn't help her balance—he kept hold of her by her waist.

"I just need a soda," she said. "Can someone get me that? I'm thirsty and I'm sure that will settle my stomach, too."

"Ginger ale," Ina said, reaching for the refrigerator door. "I read that's good for an upset stomach."

Genevieve had stopped listening and was frowning at Marshall. "What are you doing here?"

"We have a dinner date for tonight." He frowned with increased concern. This was totally unlike her. She was a master of details and schedules. She had more data in her head than his BlackBerry possessed. "If you tell me that you don't remember that, I'm taking you straight to the hospital."

His response won murmurs of approval from the two women still hovering nearby. But with a warning glance from their boss, Ina handed over the soda to Genevieve and followed Raenne out of the room.

"Raenne," Genevieve called after the other blonde. "The Bigelows have accepted your clients' offer. I'll have the paper ready for you to fax in a few minutes."

"I'll call and tell them, but take your time. Or better yet, let me do it for you. Just holler."

Now alone with her, Marshall noted that Genevieve avoided eye contact by fighting the screw top on the small bottle. "You're not going to get away with not answering the question."

"I remember dinner, but I thought I was going to meet you somewhere or—"

"We're traveling in two cars? Am I still supposed to be a secret?" He took the bottle from her and opened it with a simple twist.

"Of course not."

But she sounded less than convincing, and when he handed the bottle back to her, she murmured her thanks and eased around him to make a beeline for her office. Determined to learn what else was going on, he followed. Once inside the room, he was relieved to see that at least she sat down behind her desk, although he suspected that she did it to get more space between them.

He eased the door closed and leaned against it crossing his arms. "Hard day?"

"This contract evens things out. As you heard, Raenne and I have another sale."

"Congratulations."

"Thanks." After taking a sip of the soft drink and grimacing, Genevieve pressed a hand to her flat tummy. "I don't think I can do tonight, Marshall."

"Could it be something you ate?"

"Actually, I didn't eat—and don't start." She held up her hand as soon as he opened his mouth to protest. "I didn't eat because anything I considered made me feel queasy, okay?"

"This keeps getting better and better," he said, folding his arms across his chest. "Have you considered taking a few days off? Humans do now and then."

"I will around the holidays when it gets quiet. It's

not like I'm not doing anything different than I usually do." Genevieve tried to take another sip of the soda, but shuddered and replaced the cap instead.

"Then why don't we reschedule the dinner out and I'll go to the market and pick up a few things and make you a nice beef vegetable soup? Maybe potato cheddar and some fresh bread from the bakery? I'll even make it at your place so you can get into something comfy and warm and go to sleep right afterward?"

"That's too much trouble. I can open a can."

Marshall couldn't resist raising an eyebrow, especially since she continued to avoid eye contact. "So it's okay for you to work yourself sick on my behalf, and I can't do something that I could almost do in my sleep?"

She covered her face with her hands for several seconds, leaving Marshall to wonder if she was going to burst into tears, order him out or get sick after all. But in the end, she simply reached for her purse. Taking out her wallet, she opened the coin section and took out a single key and offered it to him. "It's an extra I carry in case I lose my keys. Please don't go overboard. I should be there—" she checked her watch "—in an hour."

"If you feel even remotely unable to make the drive," he replied, "call and I'll come get you."

The grocery store was only around the corner, so within fifteen minutes Marshall was in her house and unpacking his purchases. In another fifteen, he had onion, celery, carrots and parsley chopped, and a package of chicken thighs braised and now cooking in delicious broth. He'd opted for chicken because of the old adage about the emotional as well as physical attributes that had been passed down for generations—and because it would be ready fairly soon.

That still left him with a fifteen-minute-or-so wait for Genevieve, so he poured himself a glass of wine from the bottle in the refrigerator and took a stroll to get a feel of her home. He'd liked the outside with its other-generation charm and the landscaping. Potted plants full of vibrant pink-and-red geraniums added lively color to the green-and-white theme. Inside, he discovered she liked Eastern influences amid furniture that was either upholstered in ivory or camel, or was trimmed in rattan. A black lacquered chest was stunning in the entryway adorned with a bonsai tree that got just enough light from the glass door and humidity from a softly trickling fountain to create a mini garden oasis, whose serenity spilled into the living room. There was no formal dining room, and only three bedrooms—one of which was empty; the other was set up as an office. The master bedroom was more classical with a sleigh bed, an equally hefty armoire and two nightstands.

There was no missing the photos of her late husband. Adam had been a handsome young man in an athletic, somber way, his jaw square, his nose and brow bold and straight, his hazel eyes making no mistake who had been holding the camera—or who he'd been thinking of. Marshall went from picture to picture, room to room, to gauge his competition. He didn't want to think of that dedicated soldier as that, but there was no way around it. This was the man Genevieve had loved and had stayed faithful to for all this time despite knowing he would never come back. If Adam had lived, there would be no way Marshall would be standing here. Even now, she was protecting what had belonged to Adam. Marshall understood if he wanted to pursue these feelings he had for her—and he fully intended to—he had to make a place in her heart for himself.

How old would Adam be now if he'd lived? His own thirty-eight? Marshall guessed within two or three years of that. But in character there was no doubt they'd been as different as night and day. Genevieve had said Adam had been intent on being a career soldier. Unless there had been a draft, that was not for him, although Adam and men like him deserved and had his respect.

The sound of a vehicle had him returning to the kitchen. When Genevieve entered, she gave him an uncertain smile, her eyes darting around, including into the living room, giving Marshall a fair idea of what she was thinking. Not only was she gauging all he'd accomplished, hindsight had her remembering things—like those photos—she might have preferred he didn't see.

"It smells good in here," she said, closing the door after herself and setting her things on a small desk near the door.

"How are you feeling now?" he asked. "You don't look as pale. Do you think you could handle a sip of wine?"

"Probably not. But that bread looks and smells heavenly."

He'd stopped by the bakery and picked up a fresh loaf of simple rye. "I'll cut you a slice. The soup needs another thirty or forty minutes. Why don't you change and settle somewhere comfortable?"

She stood like a stranger in her own home, uncertain and almost shy. "Okay. It is good of you to do this."

"I'll let you in on a little secret—it's a nice change of pace to be the helper instead of being the one in need."

Watching her retreat to her room, Marshall yearned to follow her and do whatever he could to make her feel better. But he could see she was too unwell to wage a battle of wills at the moment. For the time being, he had to engage in an undeclared truce. Funny considering there was no declared war between them.

When she returned, she wore emerald-green velour sweats and thick white socks. With her hair loose from its casual chignon and brushed straight, makeup worn off and her jewelry gone, she looked about eighteen.

"Want to settle on the couch and I'll bring you a tray?"

"No, this is fine." She pulled out a chair at the breakfast-nook table.

With some help about where silverware and dishes were located, Marshall cut and warmed a slice of bread and spread a dollop of the chive butter he'd whipped up on it.

"I like your house," he said, placing the saucer before her. He added a napkin on the side from the holder on the counter.

"It must seem small compared to yours," she said. "And it's aging."

Marshall shrugged. "How much room do you need? You don't seem to spend much time here anyway. What's more, all houses are an ongoing expense. Repairs and improvements are the other side of investment. From what little I've seen, this one seems in pretty good condition."

"I do try to deal with things before they grow into

issues." She reached for half a slice, tore off a corner and slipped it into her mouth. She chewed as though she had been denied the flavor for years. "Emily Post once said that 'bread is like dresses, hats and shoes…in other words, essential.'"

"Wolfgang Puck said to go home and pound some dough in your kitchen and find out what tasty therapy it can be," he countered.

"Why did I try to impress you with my one food quote?"

"It was a good one," he said. "There's a Yiddish proverb that claims 'love is like butter—it's good with bread.'"

The slice fell out of her hands and fell facedown on the plate. "Oh, clumsy me. I should be wearing a baby bib."

"Speaking of different cultures," Marshall said, unable to resist teasing her a bit, since it seemed to be getting her mind off feeling ill, he continued, "I like the bonsai in the entryway and the Asian styling for that matter. I heard you need to be extra good with plants to keep those things alive."

"Well, they're not like cacti. You can't ignore them and expect them to thrive. I had several die on me before I caught on somewhat. The one there now is only five years old. It barely qualifies as bonsai. Finding the right fountain was key. Otherwise I couldn't hope to mist the plant enough times in one day to give it adequate humidity."

"And the decorating style?"

Her smile was weak, but wry. "That's easy. You've seen my mother's house with all the gilding and French filigree. Don't misunderstand, it's beautiful in its own way, but it would look ridiculous in rooms as small as mine—or a house that's more contemporary like yours. And, too, there are so many houses decorated just like that around here. Mother likes her friends to emulate her."

"I could have guessed that."

Waving the dainty piece of the bread she'd just torn off, she said, "I wanted something less, 'Look at me, I'm wealthy,' if you know what I mean. Growing up fascinated with books like Clavell's *Shogun* and *Tai-Pan* made me look into Eastern design. Oh, and the newer one—*Memoirs of a Geisha*. I think the style brings a serenity into a room that's helped me cope through tougher times."

"And the bread? Is it helping?"

She moaned softly. "This is a lifesaver."

Marshall leaned against the counter content to watch her sit cross-legged on the chair. There was no missing that she relished tearing the bread bit by bit with her fingers and then licking the lingering flavor of the chive butter off her fingertips. He doubted that her mother would approve, but he did. Eating was a sensual experience to him and he felt an automatic kinship with people who lingered over each bite. It pleased him to no end to discover Genevieve was one of those.

"How are you about camping?" he asked. "Were you a Girl Scout?"

"Mother would have had a stroke if I'd asked to do that. But I did take riding lessons for almost two years. That had her daydreaming about having an Olympian equestrian in the family, but when my trainer kept me on trail rides instead of in the jumping and dressage rings, mother put an end to both of our fantasies."

"Why?"

"By then I was almost seventeen and he was twenty."

"Did she have cause to worry?"

"Maybe." Genevieve offered a one-shouldered shrug. "I wasn't paying as much attention as I probably should have. I was just thrilled with any and all of the time I could spend with my horse."

Marshall threw back his head and laughed with sheer pleasure. "I do believe you were that oblivious." He had the strongest urge to take her into his arms until she held him with her thighs as though on her mount. For both of their sakes, he went to stir the soup. "Did you get through high school that unaware of what a temptation you were? Did you even go to the prom?"

"No, I was still dealing with the trauma of losing my father, mother's dating and the quickie marriage and divorce that followed. I didn't talk much at all. It took a sorority invitation in college to make me realize that unless I wanted to relocate and start from scratch, I needed to embrace my mother's increasing fame and the political-business networking structure that has become our not-so-subtle caste system."

"You've adapted well enough without selling out your principles."

She cast him an enigmatic look. "I'm more of an actor than I let Mother or anyone see. The rest is hard-won etiquette."

So she hadn't healed anywhere near as much as she let on to others, Marshall thought, taking a sip of his wine.

She retained emotional fractures, wounds that made her sadder than most people would probably guess. He could change that if she let him.

As she swallowed the last bite of bread, he asked, "Ready for another slice? The soup won't be ready for at least fifteen minutes."

"I'll try to wait. I feel stabilized," she added, rubbing her tummy. "I don't want to push my luck." A small silence ensued before she ventured, "Did you spoil Cynthia this way?"

He supposed he should have expected the question, but he'd been too preoccupied on how to broach questions about Adam to prepare himself. "Do you see this as some kind of knee-jerk reaction?" he asked.

"Maybe I am sick—or else you give me too much credit," she began. "Remember, I work with a divorcée, another widow—and Ina isn't all that sorry about that—and a woman who might as well be either. I wouldn't recognize knee-jerk if I saw it. I was just wondering about your marriage."

"What a coincidence. I wonder about yours." He waited for some facial expression or stiffening to indicate he'd approached no-man's-land, but when that didn't happen he grew more serious. "I tried in the beginning. But Cyn didn't care about food. And she liked how thin she stayed as a smoker." Feeling a bitterness rise in him at the waste of it all, he said, "Maybe we'd better table that subject for another day. Tonight, I think you should try to simply get over whatever it is that's trying to knock you off your feet."

"It is disconcerting," she said, looking as if her head was becoming too heavy for her neck. "I'm usually like you, I don't get sick. Maybe a half-baked case of the sniffles every other year or so, that's it. I barely suffer from spring or autumn allergies."

"It would seem you're pushing your luck. And I'm feeling increasingly guilty for the role I played in that."

As he talked, she seemed to finally realize there was only one place setting. "Aren't you going to eat, too?"

"I wasn't sure you'd want me to."

"That would be more than rude, that would be unkind. After you've gone to all this trouble for me?"

"It took less time for me to get this simmering than it does for you to explain points to prospective buyers and sellers." But Marshall was thrilled that she expected him to stay. "Are you sure I can't pour you a small glass of wine?"

She scrunched up her nose. "My insides rebel at the mere mention of that. But help yourself. Is it even drinkable? I thought it was okay, but I've never tried South African wine before."

"Bravo for experimenting. This chardonnay is almost past its prime, but with some fruit and cheese, most people would never know it."

By the time he served the soup, it was dusk. Marshall suggested they avoid the harsh fixture light and lit the single candle Genevieve kept in a brass enameled holder on the counter using the disposable lighter she directed him to. He placed it in the center of the table.

"It's not exactly the dinner I had planned, but it's easier on your eyes and my laugh lines," he teased.

"So much so that if it gets any more relaxing, you're going to have to fish my head out of my bowl." But after a careful taste she made a sound of pleasure. "And to think I passed on canned soup for this."

"Maybe Santa will be generous at Christmas."

They ate in companionable silence for a bit. It felt good. Right. Then out of the clear blue, she floored him with a question.

"I guess you're going to be polite and not mention all of the pictures? You did look around beyond the living room, didn't you?"

He tried to be honest without saying everything he felt. "I looked."

Genevieve kept her gaze in the almost empty bowl. "Avery calls this the Tomb of the Known Soldier."

"For all of her sharp edges, anyone can see that she genuinely cares and worries about you."

"I guess what I'm trying to say is if I'd known I was going to get sick and that you would be coming—"

Marshall reached across to cover her hand with his and stop her from saying something that wasn't totally in her heart. "The photos weren't a surprise. Intimidating, yes. Most people look good in uniform, but he was— what's the word? *Buff.* On the other hand, if you'd hidden them and Avery or your mother or anyone asked my reaction later, I'd have been more troubled that you felt the need to hide them from me." Then he would forever be wondering when they were apart if she was looking at them instead of thinking about him.

"I'm so confused, Marshall."

"I know, sweetheart." And there wasn't a damned thing he could do about it to help her. The memory of Adam was one thing she had to resolve herself. "Let it go tonight. You're really not well. It means a great deal that you wanted to share what you did."

She seemed to quit fighting her fatigue after that. Concerned that she would drop the spoon and splatter herself and everything around her, Marshall took it from her.

"What?" she asked, rousing.

"You're heading for bed."

Lifting her into his arms, he carried her to the bedroom. He liked that she accepted that and rested her head against his shoulder, liked how right she felt in his arms. But he already knew that.

Sitting her on the edge, he turned down the blue and gold patterned comforter and ivory sheets, and then slipped her between them.

"Socks on or off?"

"Mm."

"Poor exhausted darling." He covered her and kissed her forehead, then her lips more gently. "Try to pay attention. I'm going to put away everything in the kitchen except a small container of soup for you to warm up if you wake in the middle of the night. If you don't, toss it down the drain in the morning, understood? Don't risk food poisoning on top of everything else."

With a content sigh, she rolled into a relaxed fetal position. "Okay."

"Do you mind if I keep the key one more day? If you need anything, I want you to call me and be able to get in."

"Okay."

"Will you miss me?"

"Okay."

Tucking the blankets around her, Marshall kissed her once more, then left before she destroyed what was left of his ego.

When Genevieve woke it was dark except for a faint glow coming from elsewhere in the house. She didn't remember getting into bed and she missed the night-light being on in her bathroom. As she lay there and thought harder, it came to her.

Marshall had been here. He'd made soup.

Reassured, she rolled over ready to go back to sleep, but her mind started cranking images and thoughts as it often did when she went to bed too early and had succeeded in getting just enough rest to make more sleep impossible.

A glance at her clock told her it wasn't yet one o'clock in the morning. More bad news. That was way too early to be up and about. By midmorning, she would be dragging and yearning for a nap. Worse yet, she was hungry again.

What kind of bug made you sick as a dog half the time and starving the rest?

She threw back the covers and went to the kitchen, where she turned on the breakfast-nook chandelier, nuked the soup Marshall had left out for her and carried it to the table. Sitting down, she decided this was as good a time as any to browse through her mail, something she hadn't had time to do in two days.

Most of it was advertisement, but a magazine she'd picked up the other day and added to the heap had one of her favorite actresses on the cover. She paged through the glossies of airbrushed models and ads for everything from deodorant to pregnancy kits until she found the page with the feature on the actress she admired. One paragraph into the story, Genevieve froze, then flipped pages back to the pregnancy-kit advertisement.

"No!" she whispered. "Oh, *no*."

Chapter Five

During the last full week of September, only three days after she'd sat at her kitchen table and felt her axis tilt as though the earth had experienced the mother of all earthquakes, Genevieve drove to a Wal-Mart in another county and bought tissues, pantyhose, shampoo, bananas, two pumpkins for the front entryway of her house, and a pregnancy kit. As she placed it into her basket, she assured herself that she was wasting time and money and that she would probably start her menstrual cycle on the way home. When had she ever been regular anyway? Okay, since Adam, she amended. She eased that old pang of pain by thinking that this would make a good laugh at some distant point in time.

Fat chance.

Her own inner logic didn't miss an opportunity to make her feel the fool. She'd been sick as a dog for days—so much so that not only were Marshall, her

mother and the girls in the office begging her to go see
her doctor, but she was almost ready to surrender to a
physical herself, despite having had one in the spring. So
why go through the extra expense of a pregnancy kit?

Because she'd had enough surprises and shocks to last
two lifetimes. She wanted to go into an exam already
knowing that she was about to finish losing her mind,
her privacy, her reputation—basically, her life as she
knew it.

Having told Ina that she would be tied up until early
afternoon, she drove home and carried her purchases
inside. Her BlackBerry had chirped, beeped and vibrated
repeatedly throughout the morning. She ignored everything including client calls. Most of them were requests
to schedule or reschedule viewings that she would deal
with shortly.

Leaving everything but the kit on the breakfast table,
she hurried to the bathroom and ripped it open and tried
to focus on the directions. Of course, nothing made sense.
By the time she reread it for the third time, she thought
she would explode if she didn't relieve her bladder.

Afterward she made herself leave the room and get
busy putting away the rest of her purchases and placing the pumpkins out front. Her nerves couldn't handle
standing by and watching the clock. Nevertheless, the
"what if?" question kept popping into her mind like the
most elementary and irritating video game.

Finally, unable to wait any longer, she returned to the
bathroom and looked at the results. Weak-kneed, she
slumped down on the rim of the bathtub.

Genevieve didn't know how long she stayed like that,
but it eventually registered through her shock that the

light coming through the bathroom window was a fraction of what it had been. There had been more beeps and rings signaling that people were trying to call her. But she hadn't yet been ready to deal with them.

As she struggled to find the strength, she heard a totally different sound—that of the back door opening. She knew she had locked it.

Only Marshall had her key.

"Genevieve?"

He called to her once more and proceeded to come looking for her, ultimately stopping in the doorway of the master bathroom. It was nothing compared to his majestic his-hers suite, but she doubted he was thinking about that considering the way he murmured, "Thank God."

She remained hunkered over, elbows on knees, head in her hands, her hair gaining her some privacy, but not enough…and the mantra, *"Why?"* running over and over in her head.

"Genevieve, do you realize how worried everyone is about you?"

His voice wasn't angry or accusatory, it was entreating. But when she didn't so much as budge, he stepped into the room.

"Okay, this is getting scary. We've let you have your way, now we have to get you to the hosp—"

He must have spotted the box and paraphernalia on the vanity counter, especially the telltale gizmo that was their generation's equivalent to the dead rabbit in her grandmother's time. When the silence became one ounce of pressure too much, she looked up to see he had a wondrous look on his face.

She burst into tears.

* * *

For hours Marshall had been worrying about her—ever since he'd called the office this morning and been told she would be out until later. She'd been avoiding his calls all weekend and hadn't sung in the choir on Sunday. That much he'd gleaned from Bart, who was concerned himself. The few times he did get hold of her on the phone, she'd claimed she couldn't talk to him other than to blurt out in haste, "I'm sorry. I'll get back to you." The problem was, she never did.

This afternoon when he'd called the office and Ina said, "Mr. Roark, I was about to ring you to ask if you'd seen her," he'd been filled with concern, which had mushroomed into all-out dread. Fearing illness or a kidnapping, and scenarios that had grown progressively worse as the day drew on, he knew what he had to do. He let it be known to Ina that he had the key to Genevieve's house—fully knowing how upset Ina's boss would be when she found out. The thing was, he had to find her alive for her to have the luxury of taking her anger on the chin.

Now he stood before the explanation of what all of the evasive tactics and raw nerves were about.

He went to her and dropped to his knees so he could draw her into his arms. "Genevieve...sweetheart, don't. It's all right."

"No, no, no."

"Of course it is. Did you think I wasn't going to be happy? My Lord, it's *wonderful*."

That declaration turned her tears into heart-wrenching sobs as she fought to curl tighter and tighter into herself.

Her reaction distressed him and he tried to soothe her, stroke her hair and kiss wherever he could. "I should have guessed this was the problem, but I couldn't get past the fear that you were seriously ill."

"I might as well be."

"Don't say that!" Did she forget who she was talking to? What was more, she had already given him his joy of life again, real hope for the future instead of feeling as if he was going in circles or, worse yet, drowning. Her news made him want to throw his head back to thank heaven and crow to the universe.

But it was clear that she was as heartsick at the idea of a child as her body was physically rebelling against the pregnancy. He understood that the latter was due to hormones, and the former with the loss of her husband, but it wasn't in his proactive personality to wait for things to evolve on their own.

"All you need to know," he began in all earnestness, "is that no matter what, I am here for you."

Genevieve rubbed her fingertips against the smooth skin between her eyebrows. "I know you mean well," she replied, enunciating carefully. "But you're not helping."

"I thought you'd be relieved."

She made a sound as though something inside her was ripping in two. "How can I be? This is a travesty."

"What did we do wrong but find comfort in each other's arms and relief from our long emptiness?"

"I was supposed to already *have* my baby! I begged him to leave me pregnant, and I prayed that I was. I prayed so hard."

Marshall knew she wasn't intentionally trying to hurt

him, but her words wounded nonetheless. She was disappointed that the tiny flutter of life in her womb wasn't Adam's, instead of his.

"It's not fair," Genevieve continued as though alone. "One time. One insane time!"

It crossed Marshall's mind that plenty of men would see this as the smart time to cut out and lie low. But not him. While her painful outbursts were almost unbearable to listen to, and her frankness pretty well decimated him, one fact remained. *They* had made that baby. And he wasn't a quitter.

He settled beside her on the throw rug, his back against the tub, his arms resting across his raised knees. "What we did may have been premature," he began. "But I refuse to regret it."

"Good for you." Rising as though she couldn't bear his close proximity, she tossed her crumpled tissues into the trash and grabbed a new handful from the box on the counter. "In the meantime I'll be on the receiving end of stares and gossip. I'm the widow who acted like a slut with a man who just buried his wife. There's no telling how many listings this will cost me. I'll be lucky if I don't get kicked out of choir!"

"No one needs to know."

She shot him a give-me-a-break look. "How does that work? Baby bumps can't be hidden for long, especially with my wardrobe."

True, her slim sheaths, tailored suits and pencil skirts would define the obvious, but that was not what he meant. "Genevieve, what I'm saying is, by then we'll be married."

"Just like that?"

Having concluded that she didn't want any part of romance right now, he figured that exhibiting strong pragmatic thinking would gain a better reaction. "It takes care of two important issues—the baby's security and gossip."

"We barely know each other. We're certainly not in love."

Marshall wondered how she would react if he admitted to being on his way there and had been for some time. What was more, he knew she was at least physically attracted to him. Quite a bit, he amended—and that wasn't merely his trampled ego talking. If he knew anything about Genevieve Gale, it was that she would never be the loose woman she dreaded being labeled as. She had to have some feelings to be intimate. That was a start as far as he was concerned. An appealing one.

"What's more," she continued when he merely stood watching her unravel, "I have a house, you have a house—"

"We'll sell yours."

"I happen to love my house. Sell your house."

"But there's more room in mine—space for a nursery and an office for you." No sooner did he speak than he saw her square her shoulders and lift her chin.

"More isn't necessarily more."

Bad move, Roark, he warned himself and immediately backpedaled. "There's truth in that. What would be your solution?"

"I don't know," she wailed. "I'm not ready to *have* this conversation."

At least she wasn't crying her eyes out as she had been.

"Then let me get one more thing said," he began. "I've always wanted children."

Genevieve hid behind her tissues for several seconds before curiosity won out. "Why didn't you?"

Given that she wasn't at her most receptive, he took his time formulating his reply. "I'd already broken my own promise not to marry Cyn until she quit smoking. I wasn't going to have a child's health or its future with its mother compromised by that."

Genevieve's expression was on the verge of being censorious. "She must have been devastated by that decision."

"You'd be wrong. In the end she was relieved and said as much. It was one of the things that helped me get through that time." Accepting that he had to return to that painful time in order to move forward, he said, "Cynthia lost her twin brother when they were teenagers. He took his own life. Eventually she and I had to accept that she would never get over that, or be able to have a mature and complete marriage with me."

"I'm sorry." Suddenly Genevieve didn't seem to know where to look. "I had no idea."

"You weren't supposed to. No one was." He wanted to get up and take her into his arms. He hadn't meant to make her uncomfortable, just to correct preconceptions and clear up misconceptions. "Bryan had issues with their father, but I don't think anyone ever understood the full extent of his problems. Afterward, Cynthia spent the rest of her life feeling like half a person, forever anxious and trying to fill the gaping hole Bryan left in the family, which was impossible, since her father believed if anyone had been expendable in the family it was her."

Genevieve gasped. "How horrible. And the cigarettes eased her anxiety."

Marshall shrugged. "Cigarettes, alcohol, drugs du jour or prescriptions. As she beat the others, smoking became a stronger crutch. In the end it was the one thing she couldn't shake."

"Yet, she still wanted to be buried back with her family?" Genevieve asked.

"With Bryan. It took considerable persuasion, but her ashes are with him now."

Genevieve turned away and took up the washcloth folded neatly on the vanity counter. Wetting it, she covered her face. She stayed like that for several seconds before rinsing the cloth and replacing the soothing compress on her feverish and tearstained face. "I appreciate what it cost you to go over that again, and to live with such disappointment," she said at last.

"I hated sharing such grim details when you're already upset." Marshall gave her what privacy he could by gazing down at his tightly clasped hands. "But you deserved to know."

Laying the cloth on the sink's edge, she faced him. "I needed to know, but strangely it doesn't change anything."

That had his breath stalling in his lungs. "What's that supposed to mean?"

"Cynthia wasn't the only casualty in your marriage. You paid a price and I'm not sure you realize the size of it. You're not ready to jump into another relationship. I've heard psychologists say that you should wait one year for every five years you were married before entering another legal union."

Did she think he wanted to wait until their child was practically in preschool? "That's the thing about theories—life tends to circumnavigate them...when it's not turning them into fertilizer." Seeing that she didn't care for his reply, he added quickly, "It's not that I don't recognize we'll have challenges—"

"Marshall," Genevieve interjected wearily, "I'm dealing with a shock that is going to change my life. Again. I need to think, and I can't do it with you here."

She left the room, leaving Marshall with no choice but to follow. It didn't sit well to be summarily dismissed, but he knew neither of them was reacting appropriately at the moment. They were both suffering from information overload.

"Will you at least call the office and let them know you're all right? When I told her that I'd be checking things out over here, Ina asked me to let her know what I learned."

Halting in the middle of the kitchen, Genevieve looked ready to flee back to the bathroom, this time to be ill. "They know you're here?"

"They were glad to hear from me. You've been acting stranger than when you had the bug that we now know was morning sickness."

"*Is.*"

Unable to contain the joy bursting from every vein and pore, Marshall sighed. "Ah, Genevieve, all I'm saying is that now would be as good a time as any for them to realize there's a man in your life." Coming toward her, he stopped only to slip his arm around her waist to draw her close, closer, until they were pressed abdomen to arousal. "Whatever you decide, know this—I'm not going away any more than that fetus in your womb is going to stay the size of a pinhead. Think about it. And while you're at it, think about this."

Lowering his head, he kissed her as if his life depended on it.

It did.

Genevieve listened to Marshall drive away, her legs still too weak to rise from the chair she'd collapsed into when he'd finally released her. He'd certainly had his say.

He'd frustrated and troubled her as much as he'd sent her hormones into havoc, but he was right about her having stayed in poor communication with the girls at the agency.

She reached for her BlackBerry and rang the office number and breathed deeply, hoping she could be as calm and reassuring as she needed to be.

Ina must have been watching the keyboard because the first ring had only started when she pushed the line button.

"Thank you!" she declared as soon as she lifted the handset. "Do you know we were debating calling the police?"

"What did you three do, flip a coin—heads it's Marshall, tails it's 911?"

"So Mr. Roark found you?"

"I wasn't exactly lost."

"He's a nice man and he cares about you very much. How are you? You don't sound like yourself."

And probably never would again, Genevieve thought, but forced herself to look at things from her receptionist's perspective. "I'm okay, just a bit nasally. I'm sorry for making you worry. Is everything and everyone okay over there?" The best way to keep attention off her was turn it back onto the office.

"Sure. Except for people whose calls you're not returning. Hint, hint."

"That's the other reason we're talking," Genevieve said. "I need you to do that for me." She went through the list of people she wanted to reschedule. "Any questions?"

"Only a dozen. I'll edit them down to one—when do we see you again?"

"Tomorrow. I'm pretty sure I'll be back on track by then." Now that she knew what "ailed" her, she could work to keep symptoms under control...after she did some online research. She wasn't yet ready to confide in friends and employees any more than she was ready to disclose anything to the general public.

"Did you hear that?" Ina said above chatter in the background. Then she giggled. "That was Avery saying that we can buy you more time if you're contagious."

Genevieve replied, "I think you're safe. But thanks again for keeping things operational so well."

"Not so fast," Avery said, getting on the line. "Are you sure you should get back yet? You're sick, right? You didn't take off to have some plastic surgery done or a boob job?"

That woman, Genevieve thought. She really should pair her up with her mother. Too tired to think up a better comeback, Genevieve simply replied, "I think I'm finally developing what you all complain about in the autumn and spring—allergies."

"Uh-huh. Taking anything?"

"You know I don't like pills."

"What did Roark-the-licious think the problem was?"

Avery was too sharp for her own good. "Did you get the contract on the Merriman house?" she asked instead.

"You must be feeling better. You're dodging questions as well as you ever did. Merriman—we're doing a second viewing tomorrow morning. And I got a referral today for a nice little two thousand square footer that should last about twenty-four hours after we put it online and stick the sign in the yard."

"That's what I like to hear. And Raenne?"

"Poor sweetie…her great white fisherman stepped on a rusty nail left by their roofing people and she's getting him through a visit to E.R."

It wasn't long ago that Raenne's husband, Rick, went crazy with a staple gun on their wind-damaged roof and stapled his thumb to the shingles. The man was a danger to himself out of a bass boat. And expensive. "It's a wonder he didn't fall off the roof."

"It's a wonder he got up the ladder in the first place," Avery countered.

"Did she have to reschedule a closing?"

"Thankfully nothing is pending in that department before Wednesday next week."

Feeling her tummy rebel from the stress of trying to stay upbeat, Genevieve wished them a good night and disconnected. It was a relief to have that over with for the moment, but she really needed to call her mother, who was thoroughly capable of calling Marshall should the mood suit her.

Sydney picked up immediately. "Darling, what on earth? This is the longest you've been out of touch since—well, too long."

She'd almost said, "Since Adam died," and Genevieve was grateful she'd caught herself in time. No need to assist her mother in dissecting and performing psychotherapy on her life. "I apologize for that."

"When I last called your office Ina thought you caught a bug. Did you go see Dr. Kelly for a shot and antibiotics?"

"Oh, I wasn't that far gone." Except emotionally. "I took a relaxing drive in the sunshine without once looking at property and had a couple of lazy naps." The sun had been shining, she told herself, so it wasn't a total fib, and actually the soup Marshall made her was healing.

"Excuse me? The last midday nap you had was the day I stopped breast-feeding you."

Good grief, Genevieve thought, resting her head in her hand. She did not have the strength for this now. "Mother, you never breast-fed me. Are you getting me confused with one of your fictional children again?"

"The point is," Sydney replied with a note of haughtiness, "as soon as you started on solid foods, you kept the hours of a Wall Street workaholic—alert and checking on me and everything else in the house from seven to seven, then sleeping like your crib was wired to our bed, reacting to the slightest creak."

"Too much information, Mother."

"A fact of life," Sidney replied. "I only hope I'm still alive when you learn that."

"Me, too. But only so I get to hear how you explain to a toddler that you're too young to be called Grandmother or Nana and want to be called Aunt Sydney."

"Exactly why did you ring me?" Sydney drawled. "Like you, I do have a day job."

The words stuck in Genevieve's throat. "I wanted to tell you…well, funny that you were just mentioning…" She couldn't do it over the phone. "Do you want to have lunch in the next few days?"

Brightening, Sydney replied, "Why that's lovely, dear. Better yet, let's have another foursome dinner with Marshall. That went well, didn't it? Even Bart likes him, and you know how protective he is of you."

"Give him my love. Umm…let's make it just the two of us this time, okay?"

"If that's what you want. Tomorrow would be perfect for me."

"See you at noon."

"Are you sure you don't want to tell me something now? You sound a bit—stressed."

Genevieve had learned to avoid "the whole truth and nothing but" with her since before she'd graduated from high school. "You complain that we never talk enough," she demurred, "and just when I try to block you some time—"

"Okay, okay." Sydney could be heard tapping a pen on her desk blotter. "Does tomorrow make me sound too anxious?"

"Works for me," Genevieve said with forced enthusiasm.

"Do you want me to meet you somewhere or will you pick me up?"

"I thought I'd pick up something and bring it to you."

"I see. You really do want to talk. Well, why don't I have Dorothy prepare something for us then?"

"My treat. Holler if your schedule changes," Genevieve said, neither affirming or denying the intent of her visit. "I will, too. Bye."

It was a terrible way to end a conversation—leave a hundred-and-one questions in her mother's mind—but she didn't see a way around that short of saying, "Wait and see." Had she tried that, her mother would make Pulitzer Prize–winning journalists look like amateurs as she sniffed out her story.

Before she lost her courage—and the last dredges of her energy—she made one more call. She keyed the personal number of her physician, Dr. Paige Kelly. She and Paige had gone to school together and had remained good friends. As she hoped, her old schoolmate knew Genevieve would not abuse a private number and called back within minutes.

"What's wrong?" were the general practitioner's first words.

"Are you on the run or can you slot me five minutes of your time?" Genevieve asked, knowing this was the one person she could confide in.

"When I see your number on my cell, you can count on it being safe. Talk."

"I need an ob-gyn's number. Someone less than local, who you respect and whose staff will keep their mouths shut."

"Genevieve." Paige drew a deep breath. "Don't tell me?"

"Yeah, go ahead and say it. I'm worse than an out-of control teenager."

"As a true friend, I can't. I'm too happy to know you actually met someone who made you feel like a desirable woman again. As your doctor, okay, you took a stupid risk. Do you at least have a sense that he's healthy?"

"Yes, that's the least of my concerns."

"That's reassuring. And the pregnancy? Are you planning on going through with it?"

Genevieve's eyes burned with new tears. "Oh, Paige. How can I not? You know my moral position and on top of that, this might be my last chance."

"At thirty? I doubt it. But good for you. I know you have the courage to get through this. So do I know the father?"

That would be *the* question for the next weeks, maybe months. "He's new in town."

"No!" Paige gasped. "That Dallas hottie—the one whose wife died not long ago?"

"Thanks, friend." Genevieve all but ground her teeth. "You've just fulfilled my worst nightmare. If you can put that together when we haven't talked in two months, my hope of keeping this under the radar for a bit is as naive as thinking Marshall won't pressure me into marriage every day until I crumble under pressure. How on earth did you hear about him?"

"I happened to spot him in the hospital a few times during those last days." Paige whistled softly. "Boy, the old adage about still waters running deep is true. You are something else, girlfriend."

"Paige, be kind. I already have morning sickness. I

thought for the first time in my life that I'd caught the flu. Don't make me vomit all over this BlackBerry."

After a wry laugh, her doctor replied, "Stock up on soda crackers and biscotti. With luck, that part of things will stop shortly. You didn't take any cold meds for those misdiagnosed symptoms, did you?"

"Nothing. I haven't even touched a glass of wine since the night it happened. I guess I did have some kind of sixth sense."

"You're going to be such a good mommy. But what's wrong if he proposes? I would think that would be a relief."

"He did. It's just that we barely know each other."

"I would say you know one important thing—he's fertile."

"Paige—"

"Okay, I'm searching through my Rolodex," Paige said, flipping cards. "Ah! I've found her. Tracy Nyland. She's our age, maybe a few years older...I remember liking her. Her office is between here and Mt. Pleasant. I'll give her a call and put in a good word for you. Got a pen?"

"Ready," Genevieve replied.

After she hung up with the ob-gyn's office, Genevieve continued to sit in her chair and felt fatigue weigh her down to where she couldn't have risen at that moment if she'd wanted to. Nevertheless, things had been set in motion. Tomorrow she would have lunch with her mother. Next week she would meet with Dr. Nyland. The baby would get the best care. It was a start.

Finally pushing herself to her feet as though she was days away from giving birth, she checked that the back door was locked and passed through the living room to check the front door before she went to lie down again. On the way her eyes met Adam's in his favorite military portrait.

"Hey, you," she murmured. "Where are you these days? I haven't felt you for such a long time. I suppose that's a sign that I should let you go and get on with things, huh? But you know I don't want to. And you probably can see what a mess I've made of my life. I'm confused and afraid, Adam. Do you even want to hear that I still miss you?"

There were no apparitions, no angels, not even voices in her head. And yet she felt only love projected from that photo. Stroking her fingers tenderly down the dress jacket of his uniform, she continued to her room.

She must have napped, but when the phone rang again she was awake and staring at the ceiling, although it was completely dark except for the night-light she'd turned on when she'd first returned to the bedroom. Caller ID told her that it was Marshall.

"You don't have to keep checking on me," she said after picking up the receiver.

"Humor me. I left you in a bad state."

Partly due to her poor behavior. "Want me to start filling out a journal as to where I am when, what I'm doing and thinking, and turn it in weekly?"

"Daily, please. With special attention to the 'what are you thinking?' part. How needy or paranoid does that sound?"

He sounded so unhappy. If he was here, she wouldn't have been able to resist sliding her fingers into his hair to soothe him. "Believe it or not, I understand."

"You do?"

The almost boyish hope in Marshall's voice tugged at her heart. "It's amazing what a nap can do for your perspective. Don't suggest that I'd taken one sooner."

"The impulse is erased from my memory banks. I'm just grateful you could get a little rest. When did you last eat?"

"Don't push your luck."

"Okay, we're tweaking the software program… tweaking…"

Genevieve couldn't help but smile. How did he do this to her? They'd almost been fighting a scant two or three hours ago. Now he made her wish he was here with her. "I was busy after you left," she told him.

"Sweetheart, not already diving back into the workload?"

"More like making calls about a certain third party."

"Anything you want to share? You have my undivided attention."

"There's a clue that you need to think about getting a life of your own," she said in all seriousness. "My real estate work kept me sane, and will again."

"I liked it better when you were about to share what happened after I left."

Now he sounded like a kid who didn't like that a bed-time story wasn't being told fast enough. "My mother and I are having lunch tomorrow. I really do think I should tell her the news first."

"Am I invited?"

"Absolutely not. It will be hard enough to tell her by myself. And that's all I'm prepared to do yet."

"Shouldn't Bart be there? He is like a dad to you."

"He's out of town and I can't risk waiting for his return, not the way gossip travels in this town."

"How do you think Sydney will take the news?"

"Well, that's why I'm telling you. I'm sure she'll find an excuse to call you—or just blatantly knock on your door as soon as I'm out of the house."

"You are going to tell her that I've already proposed marriage, yes? That woman strikes me as someone who knows her way around a .357 if the situation arises."

"It's a 9 mm." Genevieve added, "But if she's tough with anyone, it will be with me. She'll push me to accept your proposal."

"I've said from the beginning, your mother has a wisdom that transcends her modest age."

"I think I feel my morning sickness returning."

Marshall chuckled softly. "Okay, I'll quit. I'd rather talk to you than the dial tone anytime, even when you're mad at me."

"I wasn't *mad* mad," she told him. "You just drive me a little crazy."

"Let me come over and I swear I'll fix it and make it better."

He was using his best suede-leather voice on her and she was weakening fast. "This is so beyond hopeless. Okay, if you're not going to behave about anything else, listen to this please—I'm not ready for our news to go any further yet, do you understand? I'm not even telling the girls at the office."

"Say 'our' again." When she failed to humor him, he sighed. "Okay, then let me ask you this. Does that case of morning sickness you take with you everywhere know about this plan of yours?"

"I know, I know. But I have to think strong. I also made an appointment with an ob-gyn next week. My doctor here in town, Paige Kelly, recommended her. Dr. Tracy Nyland—she's out of the county."

"You have been busy."

"I knew making calls from my office wouldn't be convenient."

"So you're going back to work tomorrow?"

"If at all possible. As I told Paige, I guess I suspected for days what the real problem was, but I think denial made me get sick as much as the hormone shift did."

"I'm proud of you—and feeling a little sorry for myself. Big Daddy has no role in this operation yet."

"Big Daddy" had her pressing her lips to her mouth and tears flooding her eyes.

Marshall continued, "But I am grateful you're letting me in on things. Can I at least go to the doctor with you?"

"Not this time."

He latched on to that. "So I can ask to go the next time?"

Genevieve stroked her tummy. "Marshall, do you not realize men tend to bribe women to avoid any and all appointments with an ob-gyn?"

"That's their business—and mistake."

While her heart melted to the consistency of warm bread pudding, Genevieve grappled for some last ounces of practicality. "You know what would help enormously? A copy of your medical report. Dr. Nyland will have questions and I have absolutely zero answers."

"No problem. I actually keep a copy on file. I just have to locate the right box in my office. You've just inspired me to quit procrastinating about that part of the house. Also, if you let me know the time of your appointment, I'll be on standby and you can call and we can answer any other questions by phone. You already have the answer to the most important one. The father is thrilled."

Swallowing, Genevieve managed, "I believe you." She had to clear her throat. "Marshall…I know I've been hard on you."

"You've had every reason."

"That doesn't discount you being so understanding and patient."

"You mean I should have slung you over my shoulder and carried you back to my glass and brick cave after all?"

"Okay, go back to being patient and understanding."

Marshall chuckled. "You're going to need me, you know. You'll soon be yearning for foot rubs and back rubs, and someone to complain to at the end of the day. You don't even have a parakeet to talk to, do you?"

"I'm not home enough to have a pet."

"Well, that will change."

A mental red light flashed in Genevieve's mind. "There you go again."

He exhaled. "Medically. I was speaking about having to adapt to what's going to happen. I think—ask your ob-g-whatever—that you won't be able to keep the hours you have been. You have a little parasite sucking you dry. It seems logical that you'll have to reprogram."

"Parasite…reprogram? Marshall, say something nice so I don't have nightmares that I'm going to give birth to something out of those *Alien* movies because I'm going to hang up in five seconds."

"Dream about me watching you nurse our baby. And me holding you both as you sleep."

Along with his velvety tender voice, the sensual, romantic images worked all right, she thought as she said goodnight and hung up. Too well. Now she would do well to sleep at all thanks to him triggering her libido. And she was sure he'd done that on purpose.

Chapter Six

For her luncheon with her mother the next day, Genevieve picked up two Cobb salads at The Garden Shed, an indoor-outdoor eatery in town. It turned out to be a good idea, since Dorothy had asked for the day off to spend with her visiting grandkids. The Northeast Texas area was enjoying some lovely autumn weather, making it warm enough to eat outside, which was what Sydney had prepared for.

With no showings today and only paperwork she could catch up on this afternoon, Genevieve considered her russet suede pants suit and agreed that would be a fine idea as long as she sat under the patio table's umbrella. "I'm surprised you don't have your landscaper here already planting chrysanthemums and pansies," she said as she carried the shopping bag through to the kitchen.

Dressed in one of her ruby-red sweat suits, her mother led the way making her 18k charm bracelet jingle as she flicked her wrist. "Mr. Martinez says I need to wait one more week. This El Niño weather will supposedly play havoc with the pansies. Warmer than usual now, but colder than we need later. He said only the chrysanthemums will be happy. I think he's just buying time taking care of his commercial customers first."

As usual her mother saw a conspiracy. "Mother, your yard is gorgeous and Mr. Martinez values you as a client. With perfectly lovely flowers still going strong, why tear them out before you have to just to be the first one in the neighborhood with seasonal blooms?"

"Because I'm Sydney Sawyer and people expect me to keep to a standard." Opening the French doors to the back patio, her mother indicated the set table. "I poured us both decaffeinated sweet tea. Is that okay, or would you prefer wine? There's not much difference calories-wise, is there? But I'm working on a presentation to a women's club in Houston next week and needed a clear head."

With a private smile, Genevieve nodded. "So do I. Congratulations on that. Will you and Bart make it a mini-vacation? I'll bet he'd like to try a golf course or two while you're down there."

Drawing out two chairs from the white iron table with the hunter-green umbrella shading it, Sydney made an affirmative sound. "He's meeting one set of friends at Memorial the morning after we arrive. He has another date at Eagle Point the next day and at Oakhurst the day after that. I've a good mind to fly home and let him drive himself back—if he ever realizes that he misses me."

What was this? Sydney didn't think Bart was giving

her enough attention? "You two didn't have a spat, did you?"

"He's been so grumpy lately."

"I haven't noticed that."

"He adores you, of course he's not going to let you see anything but his Saint Bart persona. But he's complaining that I haven't cut back on my time in the office—as he claims I promised, although I don't remember any such conversation. And he thinks I meddle too much. I don't meddle. I'm interested in what people have to say."

"You meddle."

"Well, of course you'll be on his side. I don't know why I even said anything."

As Sydney unfolded her green linen napkin, Genevieve urged, "Oh, Mother, stay in Houston with him and let him show you off to his friends' wives. You know that will mean as much to him as a good day on the greens."

"I've gained six pounds with this book," Sydney muttered, "and that twenty-first-century pirate Jack Denny has taken a trophy wife. I don't need to sit across a table looking at someone that could be your twin pretending that I'm thrilled to be there."

"She can't be much of a trophy wife, Mom. Jack's been cleaned out by ex-wives three times already."

"Bless your memory, you're right! Goodness, this may be fun after all." Sydney leaned over and patted Genevieve's cheek. "Thank you for this, Gigi. I've missed our visits. Are you feeling better? You still look fragile."

Genevieve had suspected her mother's generation would be the last who could get away with using that term without sounding as though they were rehearsing a Tennessee Williams play. "I'm…regrouping and better, thanks."

"Did your doctor ever find out what the problem was?"

Taking their salads out of the bag, Genevieve placed her mother's before her and removed the clear plastic dome lid. "I did, although I don't see the doctor until next week. Here's your extra dressing, Nana."

"Oh, these Cobbs are worse than cheesecake on the thighs and derriere. If I had an ounce of restraint left in me, I'd throw out the dressing, but you know I won't. I do need the occasional sinful pleasure. I can't have my characters having all of the fun."

It took until Genevieve was opening her own dressing container that Sydney uttered a strangle-voice squeak and dropped her fork. "What did you call me?"

Genevieve shrugged. "You knew something was up."

"I suspected that you were going to take Avery as a partner, or wanted to buy a larger building. You're pregnant? *My* baby?" As soon as she finished that gush, Sydney turned worried. "It is Marshall's, right?"

Genevieve almost choked on her first bite of cracker. "Thanks for the compliment, Sydney. As I've told you before, I have nothing in common with some of the so-called heroines in your novels."

"As independent as you are, for all I know you went to a sperm donor bank before Marshall barely entered the picture." She leaned closer. "Does he know?"

Reaching for her sweating tea glass, Genevieve replied, "Yes."

"When's the wedding?"

"Marshall has asked me to marry him, but I haven't accepted." Picking up her fork, Genevieve scooped up a bit of bacon and egg, ignoring her mother's aghast expression.

"Why on earth not? I knew the man was all but besotted with you when we stopped by his house that night." Sydney gasped. "That was the night, wasn't it? You could barely look at him and he couldn't take his eyes off you. Mercy, I ran straight to my office to jot down notes."

"Have you no shame?"

Charms and earrings jangled as her mother expressed her confusion. "I just paid you a compliment."

Feeling her insides quiver, Genevieve took a few deep breaths to stave off a wave of nausea. Once more in control, she said as calmly as she could, "I haven't accepted because we have no business being married. We barely know each other. I'd have to look at his closing paperwork to remind myself what his birth date is. He doesn't have a clue as to what mine is or much of anything else."

"Except for where your erogenous zone is located," Sydney muttered, still piqued.

"Mother!"

"I like him. Gigi, the man has already proposed, what more can you ask for? If you don't accept, you'll live to regret it."

"Thanks for the support." Genevieve glared at the cube of avocado on her fork. "I can't believe you're more upset with me not immediately accepting the proposal of the man—"

"Not any man."

"—than you are that he made me pregnant."

"Well, you had a little to do with that, didn't you? And plenty have wanted to be in his shoes. The fact that you've never been tempted and this time gave in speaks volumes to me." Sydney leaned close and touched Genevieve's cheek. "My precious girl. I wish you would let yourself be happy."

"I'm not unhappy. I get to feel a deep sense of satisfaction every time I'm sitting at a closing table."

"I'm not talking about that kind of happiness."

No, she wasn't, but what her mother was referring to didn't come along very often. Probably never twice in one lifetime. "My heart was broken!"

"I understand. So was mine!"

"At least you had Daddy longer."

"Oh, and that made it easier?"

Genevieve put down her fork and folded her hands, understanding that if she didn't let her mother speak her fill, she would be hearing asides and observations from third parties for the rest of her pregnancy. "You have my attention."

"Peace of mind and the joy that comes from knowing you're with the one you should be is the kind of happiness I'm talking about," her mother began quietly. "That special someone who can make you laugh one minute and turn your knees to melting butter the next. Someone who is there with that strong shoulder on a very bad day, even when it's because of a bittersweet memory of time past. I applaud your hard work and success, Gigi, but without someone to share it with, it's a hollow victory."

"Did you just paraphrase from an old tearjerker movie?"

Sydney paused and thought. "It does rather sound like Bette Davis, doesn't it? Hell, maybe I just stole from one of my old books, I don't know. The point is such feelings cross the parameters of time."

For all of the theatrics, Genevieve knew her mother had a point. "Whatever. I didn't really come here for a pep talk. I came prepared to apologize for the embarrassment I might cause you down the road."

Sydney drove her fork into a calorie-filled cube of avocado and eyed it with relish. "You handle things the way you feel you need to. I'll be fine, and so will Bart."

Driving over here, Genevieve knew that. Sitting here now, she knew she had to tell the rest of what bothered her. "Do you understand how everything is upside down for me? This was supposed to be Adam's child. I wanted him to get me pregnant before he left for the war."

Her mother nodded, her expression turning reflective. "Such things aren't in our hands. You would have a brother or sister if it had been up to your father and me."

This was news to Genevieve. "Really? You never said anything."

"You were too young to be burdened with such things. Do you think you could fall in love with Marshall?"

She thought about what Marshall had said to her when she'd claimed they weren't in love. She *had* to have felt quite a bit to have let herself be swept away by passion. That wasn't the problem. Feeling as if she still belonged to Adam was the problem.

"He's everything you see him as," Genevieve replied. "Smart, creative, interesting."

"Darkly handsome."

"Mother, do not even consider asking him to pose for one of your book covers, let alone fantasize him as one of your story heroes. That's disgusting."

"You just said you aren't marrying him."

"I said not yet."

"I noticed how kind and attentive he was when you two came over for dinner that day," Sydney reflected.

"Oh, he is. Maybe too much." Genevieve fussed with the linen napkin lying in her lap wondering if she should say more. "Mother, it worries me that he'll treat me as though I'm another Cynthia. She needed caring for in many ways. I don't. I'll have a doctor and you to help me figure out this pregnancy, but he's already nudging me to arrange for more time off and how to arrange the nursery and my office."

"Are you putting a nursery in at the agency?" Sydney asked.

"No, my office in *his* house that he thinks I should move into."

"Ah. And did he decide what would happen to your house?"

"He's certain that I would want to sell it, since his has so much more to offer."

"It is a divine house. And yours wouldn't be practical for much longer."

"That's all well and good, but I can't finish pondering one set of his ideas before he hits me with another," Genevieve said.

"He has a great deal of time on his hands," Sydney observed. "You've given him something exciting to look forward to instead of feeling sorry for himself and mourning his late wife. Count your blessings. Many a woman would change seats with you in a heartbeat."

Despite herself, Genevieve smiled. "Yes, and three of them are in my office." Sighing, she shrugged helplessly. "He doesn't realize that we would smother each other. He needs his space and I need mine."

It was another half hour before Genevieve forced herself to leave, but she didn't get far. As she approached Marshall's property, she saw him walking to check on his mail. She knew she couldn't just wave and keep driving, so she pulled over and lowered the passenger window.

"What a coincidence, Mr. Roark," she drawled. "Are you starting to monitor the goings-on at my mother's house the way she does yours?"

Having reached the brick-encased box, he opened it and took out several envelopes. "So much for your suspicions. I think that should require a penalty. Come in for a glass of tea or—what else are expectant mothers allowed to drink?"

"My stomach can't take one more of anything, but I will come in for a second. You have a right to know that you won't have to worry about my mother coming to whip you with her Gucci bag for destroying her daughter's reputation."

She shifted into Reverse and backed enough to turn her SUV into the driveway. By the time she stepped out, he had reached her and leaned over to kiss her cheek.

"You look lovely and less stressed than you have been in a while." He extended his hand. When she took it, his smile deepened. "So lunch was easier than you thought?" As they walked, he caressed the back of her hand with his thumb. "I was hoping it would be."

"Oh, she was typical Sydney, but on the important things, she was more understanding than I deserved her to be. You'll be thrilled to know she's on your side."

"Why does there need to be sides?"

"You know what I mean."

"Okay, but your mother likes men in general, so I had a head start to begin with."

Remembering some of her comments about Marshall had Genevieve rolling her eyes. "Tell me about it. So what have you done today besides pat yourself on the back?"

He laughed as she released his hand and entered the house. "Thought about you."

"I wasn't fishing for a compliment."

After he shut the door, he turned to her and this time took both of her hands and kissed each before settling her arms around his neck. "That's not a compliment, it's a fact of life. You were already my preoccupation. Now you've become my world." Slipping his arms around her waist, he slowly drew her against him.

Feeling her body already begin to betray her as she felt his stir, she warned, "Marshall, I can't stay."

"I know," he sighed. "But you could let me kiss you properly. It's been too long and I want to hold my babies close for a few moments."

Unable to deny him a little closeness with what she would be enjoying 24/7, Genevieve let him continue to align their bodies. As she lifted her face to his, she realized that he must have shaved only a short time ago because his skin was almost smooth as he coursed a series of kisses over her lips and cheeks and chin before locking his mouth to hers for a hungrier exploration. Genevieve couldn't resist stroking his jaw and cheek any more than she could keep from arching into his arousal or matching the eager strokes of his tongue against hers.

"No changes," he said at last.

She smiled against his lips. "Silly. It will take a little time."

"One change—you aren't as skittish with me. Thank you for that."

"You know I trust you in that way—and I do want this to be all right."

"It will be." He tightened his arms and kissed her deeply again. "I want you. The problem with tasting from what's forbidden is that's all you want thereafter."

"And what got us here in this situation."

A wicked gleam lit his deep-sea eyes. "There's one point in our favor—I can't get you pregnant again."

"But I do have to get back to the office." She began to ease out of his arms.

"What's your evening look like?"

"Don't ask. I'll be catching up on paperwork for the next few evenings."

"Your nausea seems under control for now."

"That will be true if the salad I ate for lunch stays down."

"Let me come over later and cook something easy on your tummy. I want to show you what I've been working on."

Genevieve glanced around. "What have you been working on?"

"Have you got a second? Come see."

He took her hand and drew her to his office. There on a drafting table beside the big desk she saw a sketch in the works. It was a rougher plan of the house, but the focus was on two of the bedrooms on the east side. He'd removed the connecting wall and it appeared it was half office and half nursery.

"What do you think?" he asked, increasingly eager. "I know you haven't decided what to do yet, but I thought I'd show you how, when it's not mandatory for you to be at your office in town, you can still work, but in comfort here and without having to worry about what the baby is doing."

Trying to stay calm, Genevieve struggled to put humor in her voice. "And what do I tell clients when the baby is crying from colic or teething and I can't hear the caller or they can't hear me?"

"It's not like that's a long-term problem. The child will grow out of that."

"That, too. I won't always need a nursery. One day he or she will want a room alone."

"There's another bedroom for that. We don't need a guestroom, do we? Your mother isn't in need of it and I have no one left. Besides, you may have another baby."

This time Genevieve backed several feet away from him. "Marshall, stop. This is not fair. I'm still wrapping my mind around the fact that I'm pregnant. You not only have me moving in here, you're telling me how we're going to raise the child and that we're expanding the family."

He began reaching for her, only to drop his arms when she withdrew yet another step. "They're just ideas, sweetheart. Having just moved in here, I'd lose too much if I put this house up for sale again so soon. Since you've had your house for several years, it just makes more sense to sell it—plus there's the size matter. I could oversee any improvements you might want to make there. That would take any added pressure off you while you're working through your pregnancy."

"But I don't want to change anything. I love that house and I've been at peace there—something which is happening less and less here!"

Feeling her stomach warn her that conditions were deteriorating, she muttered, "I have to go."

She barely made it to the door before he called to her. "Genevieve!"

She ignored him and got as far as the front door before he stopped any further progress by flattening his hand against it. "Move, Marshall," she demanded her voice shaking. "I need to get back to the office."

"You can't go like this. You're upset."

"Of course I'm upset. I can't think or breathe!"

He stepped back as though she'd struck him. "I'm… sorry."

She couldn't bear to look at him for fear of weakening. She wished they could go back to when he'd been holding her and kissing her. Those moments were sheer bliss.

"I'll call you later," she said quickly and let herself out.

Marshall nearly became ill himself as he watched Genevieve drive away. He'd convinced himself that once she saw actual images of how he could make things look for her and their baby, she wouldn't be so confused and nervous. Instead, she'd seen him as being pushy, maybe even controlling. He was anything but—hadn't he invited her ideas? These were suggestions only. Hell, he would be happy to leave the rooms as they were if that was what she wanted. He only wanted *her.*

He went to his office and scowled at the drafting table with the drawings. *Screwup,* he thought bitterly, and ripped the sheet off the pad, crumpling it with disgust. If this had been Cynthia, he couldn't have drawn enough plans. She would contentedly let him fry every available brain cell to see what else he had to offer, but Genevieve was by no means Cynthia. She had her own mind and that mind wasn't made up yet—about him or anything about the future. Cynthia tired him. Genevieve made him feel as though he was an island tethered to the mainland in danger of being cut loose. Usually, he was a quick study of human nature. What was the problem? Genevieve wasn't a high-strung thoroughbred who needed to be handled with kid gloves, as Cynthia had been. Sensitive, yes. He'd thought he had been responding to that sensitivity.

He brooded all afternoon and paced inside and out waiting for the call that didn't come. He lifted the phone a dozen times to call her, and then another half-dozen times to order flowers for her, but the thought of what message to write on the card without starting a wildfire of gossip stopped him. Genevieve wouldn't just run from him if he brought that down on her head—she'd come after him with a carving knife.

Before he reached for his BlackBerry again, it signaled him. Seeing her BlackBerry number filled him with a strange mixture of relief and dread. "How are you?" he asked gruffly.

"I just wanted you to know that I couldn't keep down lunch. I'm going home to go to bed."

"That's my fault. Genevieve, forgive me."

"I don't want to fight with you, Marshall. It's killing me."

"Darling. Don't say that. I'm sorry. I've thrown the drawings away."

"You didn't have to do that."

"I've had nothing but time to think about it and you're right. That's a great deal of structural changes for what amounts to a short period in everyone's life. Keeping the walls as they are was smarter." When she said nothing, he realized he'd almost made another mistake. "Doing nothing right now would be smartest."

"Thank you for understanding."

He let himself take a sustaining breath. "Is there anything I can do for you?"

"Think up something to tell the girls. They're about to kidnap me and haul me to the hospital."

"If this continues much longer, I'll take you myself. You haven't kept down a full meal in days."

"I know."

Her weak reply told him that she still didn't want to deal with that. Her desire to keep everyone in the dark was impractical and could be critical if she needed sudden medical attention. But with her feeling so poorly, Marshall voiced none of that. For now that had to be his burden to carry.

"I'm beyond grateful you called," he said. "I know what it cost you. Please...I don't care what the time is, if you wake up and need something, or just can't sleep, call me."

"Why should both of us lose sleep and be miserable?"

"I'm already miserable from making so many mistakes with you."

"Oh, God. I have to go, I'm going to be—"

Marshall couldn't believe he'd been disconnected and didn't know if she'd done it on purpose or if she'd had an accident. Unable to bear the uncertainty of that, he ran for his wallet and keys and raced for his Mercedes. Considering the background sounds, he figured she had already left the office and was heading home. Had she had time to pull over before becoming ill? Did she become disorientated and have a wreck?

Tormented by his mind that pictured the worst, he drove too fast toward town, and swore when he saw flashing lights behind him. It was agony to pull over when everything in him screamed to get to Genevieve, but he hadn't lost his senses completely to risk outrunning a squad car.

To make matters worse, it turned out to be the chief himself, Phil Irvine. Grimacing, Marshall pulled out his license and proof of insurance as the steel gray–haired cop took his time approaching his window. By the time he did, Marshall had the two pieces of identification extended out the window and set his right hand on top of the steering wheel.

"Sorry, Chief. Medical emergency."

Chief Irvine took the ID and then gave him a quick study. "Roark, right? On the lake? You came into the station to introduce yourself."

"That's me."

"What's your medical emergency?"

"It's not me. It's—" well, now he'd put his foot in it "—Genevieve. She's ill and she disconnected. That's no excuse, but if you'd go ahead and write me the ticket, I really need to get to her."

"Genevieve Gale?"

"Yes."

"What's wrong with her?"

"Flu or virus…she can't seem to kick it. Please, Chief. The ticket? I'm not sure she was strong enough to drive herself home without having a wreck."

"You two an item?"

Marshall's first impulse was to reply, "You have no idea," but he had just enough sanity left to offer a respectful, "Yes, sir. We're trying to be."

"She's a nice lady. Pretty woman." The grim-faced lawman handed the ID back to Marshall. "I've never met anyone so willing to be fined. Do you think she needs an ambulance?"

"I don't know. I guess I won't until I reach her."

"Well, get moving—but stay within the speed limit. I'll be monitoring dispatch to see if you need more help."

Marshall exhaled in relief and flung the ID onto the passenger seat. "Thank you, Chief."

Genevieve must have had to pull over somewhere because she was just pulling into the garage when he turned into her driveway. Her look when she spotted him gave him another kick in the heart. He was the last person she wanted to see.

He quickly stepped out of the car and called over the coupe's hood, "Don't be afraid—or angry. You cut off so quickly, I'm only checking to make sure you made it."

She nodded weakly and turned to head indoors when she slumped against the SUV.

"Genevieve!"

He'd never moved so quickly, racing to her as she began to slide toward the concrete floor, and swept her into his arms, barely saving her from an ugly blow to the skull. Almost weak-kneed from the close call, he fought the urgent need to crush her against him.

"Hold on, baby. I'll get you inside."

By the time he unlocked her door and laid her on the bed, he had broken out in a cold sweat that had nothing to do with her near limp weight, and everything to do with his cold terror. What made matters worse was that she stayed where he put her, looking like a broken doll. For once, he willed her to move, even if it was to turn away from him and coil into a fetal position.

Struggling not to panic, he sat down on the edge of the bed and gently brushed the strands of hair sticking to her forehead. Apparently, she'd been feverish. "Genevieve, I'm going for your purse. I want to check your BlackBerry for your doctor's number."

"No…fine."

"Damn it, sweetheart, you're not. There could be complications with the pregnancy."

"No. Normal. Just…wash up."

"You're too weak to stand. You can't even form a solid sentence."

Normal…she had to be joking, and he silently berated himself for not having already looked up morning sickness online. No, instead he'd gotten carried away with the foolish nursery plans. And he couldn't do it now because he didn't know her laptop password. Considering her condition at the moment, he didn't think it would do much good to ask her for it, either. Then he thought of Sydney. He didn't expect her to have her daughter's password, but she could easily look up the subject for him.

"Tell you what." He reached to the foot of the bed and covered her with the afghan that had been lying folded there. "If you'll stay put, I'm going to get you a warm washrag, and then I'm going to make sure your car is secure and lock mine. Back in a minute."

He got her the wet cloth and left her to do what he'd said. Then he checked Genevieve's BlackBerry for her doctor's number. But Dr. Nyland was delivering a baby at the hospital.

Next he looked up Sydney's number, and used that device to call. Not surprisingly, Sydney thought she had her daughter on the line and was effusive when she answered.

"Darling, how lovely—two chats in a day. I so enjoyed our visit."

"Sydney, it's Marshall," he said quickly. "Now don't panic, but I'm at Genevieve's and she's not well."

"Good Lord. But I only saw her. She was almost the picture of health. What's happened?"

"She's insisting it's the damned morning sickness."

"She's probably right. It can be debilitating and comes and goes quickly."

"I don't mean to get personal, but did you suffer from it when you were carrying her?"

"No, bless her. My Gigi was perfect in every way."

On that they could agree. "Okay, look, I have no way of checking online right now and her doctor is in delivery. I was wondering if you'd Google the subject for me online?"

"First tell me if she's bleeding or vomiting nonstop? If there's any hint of that, forget the rest and get her to the hospital immediately."

Did she think him a complete idiot? If Genevieve had ripped a fingernail in that fall, they would already be in E.R. "No, thank God," he said with growing impatience. "But she all but fainted when she got out of the car here at her house, and I think she must have pulled over along the way to be sick."

"Poor sweetie. I suspect our lunch salad was too much for her. And considering the pace she keeps, I've been telling her to take some vitamins for ages," Sydney replied. "She's alert now, isn't she?"

Pinching the bridge of his nose, Marshall said, "That's the point. She's not. She's barely speaking fragments. And—forgive me if I'm offending you, but have you not noticed she's lost weight?"

"Of course I have," Sydney replied. "But may I remind you, Marshall, that it's you who has put her into an emotional tailspin. That said, it's not uncommon to lose a few pounds at first."

He could accept that not-so-subtle censure. "If you say so, but I can't see how that's safe for the baby."

"A fetus is a resilient little thing. Has she acted like she's cramping?"

Dear God, he thought. "She hasn't moved so much as an eyelash."

"Well, keep an eye out for that, but otherwise put some crackers within reach for her and she should probably stay off the computer and avoid TV for the rest of the day. All of that page scrolling and eyestrain can add to the nausea."

"I'd still feel better taking her to E.R."

"I understand, but unless she admits to hurting, she'll have your head if you attempt that. She wants to maintain her privacy about her condition as long as she can."

"Don't I know it," he muttered.

"And no more conversations that get her stressed."

What all had Genevieve told her mother? "It's never been my intention to do that. She's has enough of that in her life already, and any time you work with the public, that's its own potential can of worms." Sydney didn't know how fortunate she was to be incubated from that sitting in her private office as she was.

"Can you handle things there?" Sydney asked. "You aren't going to leave her alone, are you?"

"I'd like to camp out on her couch as long as she's not fully cognizant. Later if she feels stronger, though, she might have something to say about that."

"If that happens, call me back and I'll relieve you. Bart is out of town and I wouldn't mind at all."

"All right, I will. Thanks for the input," he added, although he could have done without some of her opinions.

"You're welcome. Will you give me an update when you can?"

"Of course."

As he disconnected, Marshall thought about all Sydney had said—at least about her health. A vitamin deficiency would need a doctor's diagnosis, but he could at least check what Genevieve had in her medicine cabinet to see if there was something there that would give him a clue that she was keeping from her mother.

He returned to the bedroom to check on Genevieve and found her sleeping deeply. Her coloring seemed improved and she didn't act as though she was in any new distress, so he detoured to the bathroom to check for medicines and vitamins. Finding neither, only an over-the-counter pain reliever and low-dose aspirin, he eased out of the room and went to work getting those things done that he'd promised earlier.

About a half hour later he thought of her mailbox and went out to check it. He was on his way back to the house when he spotted an elderly man with a cane exiting the house next door.

"Say there! Hold on!" the scrappy senior citizen called out.

Marshall hesitated then backtracked to meet the frail rail of a man inching along his concrete driveway. The nearly bald guy didn't look capable of making it the whole way without oxygen. "Yes, sir, can I help you?"

"You can tell me what you think you're doing," the man with the quaking voice demanded. "I've never seen you here before and I've lived on this cul-de-sac for the entire forty years since it was built. That's Genevieve's house," he added, pointing with his cane. "Where is she?"

"She's come down with a bug, sir. I'm a friend, Marshall Roark. I live by the lake two houses away from Genevieve's mother, Sydney Sawyer. Genevieve actually was the agent who sold me my property and we'd just been talking over at my place when she became ill, so I followed to make sure she was okay."

"Take her to the hospital. The mail can wait. It's nothing but medical bills and insurance advertisements anyway." Through cataract-cloudy eyes, he peered at Marshall. "You didn't give her food poisoning, did you?"

Oh, brother, Marshall thought. The old guy was overdue for a dose of his own medicine, but he didn't want to be the cause for calling 911. "Not me, sir. She'd just had lunch with Sydney."

"Who's that?"

"The writer Sydney Sawyer."

"Who's that?"

"Genevieve's mother."

"Don't know her, but you sort of sound like you do and might have a right to be here. Then again, you never can tell these days." He shook a shaky finger into Marshall's face. "Listen here, Genie is a good girl and doesn't mess around. You treat her with respect, and while you're at it, don't embarrass the neighborhood."

Coughing into his fist, Marshall nodded repeatedly. "I'll pass on your concern and best wishes, sir."

The neighborhood watchdog scowled at him from beneath wild white and gray eyebrows that would have made Medusa's head full of writhing snakes take notice. "I'll be watching to see that you leave."

"If that becomes necessary, you should watch for another vehicle. That would be Mrs. Sawyer, Genevieve's mother."

"What's her name?"

Marshall felt trapped in a Tim Burton movie...*Alice in Wonderland, Edward Scissorhands*...one of those.

"Genevieve's mother's name is Sydney Sawyer. She's a famous writer."

The squinty-eyed man with the liver-spotted face scowled back at him. "She's not too famous. I've never heard of her. Now Mark Twain, there was a famous writer."

"I'll bet you have his autograph, too."

"Say what?"

Marshall gestured with the mail. "I do need to get back inside, Mr.— I'm sorry, I didn't catch your name."

"Butler. Don't try to be a comedian. First name is Riley, not Rhett."

The old man was a fox if only a fading one. "I admire your sense of humor, Mr. Butler. Thank you for being such a good neighbor to Genevieve."

"Well, she's been an angel to the wife and myself. That's Shirley, not Scarlett. Shirl doesn't get around as well as I do and Genevieve often picks up our medications and arranges for rides to the grocery for us."

"She has spoken with affection and concern for you both," Marshall replied. "I'll go on now and see how she's doing."

"Give her our love."

Waving, Marshall hurried to the house. If the Butlers—not Rhett and not Scarlett—needed errands run from now on, he would be doing them. They weren't going to exhaust what little energy Genevieve had in reserve right now.

When he returned inside with the mail and Genevieve's purse, he set things on the kitchen table and went to see if there was any change in her condition. This time he found she had curled into a fetal position. At least it was something, but he wondered if she was cold, upset or—God forbid—cramping. Chilled, he realized, feeling her hands and finding them icy. While the temperature was comfortable for him, it wouldn't be for someone not feeling well and underweight.

It would have been best to get her into her pajamas, but not wanting to risk her reaction, he settled for taking off her shoes and easing her under the thicker comforter. Once he was reassured that she would remain peaceful, he returned to the kitchen to ring Sydney again.

"She's settled down, and seems to be sleeping more comfortably," he reported. "Since that's the case, I'll camp out on the couch, as planned. At least until she wakes again."

"That's good. I don't think it's a wise idea to leave her alone."

"Do you know her neighbors, the Butlers? I was cornered by Riley."

"Not Rhett," Sydney piped in.

"Ah. You've met the rascal."

"No. Knowing my unquenchable thirst for characters, Genevieve has imparted enough details from their conversations for me to get a vivid mental image. What about him?"

"He's hinted at calling 911 on me if I don't leave at a decent hour. My instincts tell me he's pretty harmless. He thinks he's protecting Genevieve's reputation as much as being a watchdog for his neighborhood. But I know your daughter would be mortified if I had to do a lot of explaining for a police call at this address."

"You should be all right. From what I've gathered from Gigi, his bark is always worse than his bite."

"That's what I was hoping. All right then, have a good night. It's not my plan to have to trouble you again this evening."

"Oh, do feel free. Riley Butler may not interest me overly much, but you, my boy, have my daughter's future happiness in your hands."

Chapter Seven

When Genevieve opened her eyes the room was dark and she didn't quite know where she was. Dark…the room never was, not totally. Was it even hers? That was her alarm clock on the night table. But how could it be 1:15 a.m., yet she was sleeping in her clothes?

The cobwebs of confusion cleared faster once she pushed back the covers and sat up. That was when one word formed on her lips. "Marshall."

Worried, he had come after her. If he hadn't, she could have been injured during that fainting spell. She shivered with dread as she realized she could have lost the baby. Thankfully, except for the strong desire to wash up and get out of her street clothes, she felt okay. Decent. She would have to call him so that he would know how grateful she was that he'd ignored her and come to check on her. She owed him an apology, too. She was not proud of the way she'd reacted, and she should have handled things better. The child she'd endangered was Marshall's as much as it was hers.

Once she was confident her legs would hold her, she stripped out of her things and went to the closet, where she slipped on a thigh-length ivory tunic and bikini panties. Then she went to the bathroom and switched on the night-light, which was all the help she needed to brush her teeth.

Feeling increasingly more like herself, she decided to check the house to make sure everything was locked, although she was confident Marshall would have been thorough in that respect, as well. Hopefully, he'd left her a note. She didn't deserve such a thoughtful communication, but it would give her a sense of how to start their conversation when she called him later.

While almost soundlessly padding through the near dark living room, she heard something rustle to her left. Gasping, she spun around, nearly stubbing her toe on the leg of the sofa table. On the other side of it, was Marshall, all six-two or so of him cramped impossibly on the love seat. Since her living room was on the compact size, she had purchased it instead of a full-size couch in order to have room for chairs and some accent tables.

Tiptoeing around the furniture, she leaned over until her cascading hair caressed his bare shoulder. She could see him well enough to know that he was awake and watching her. "What are you doing here?" she asked.

"Why are you whispering?" he replied in kind.

"Because...I don't know." Speaking in her normal voice, she gestured to his impossible sleeping arrangement. "You can't be comfortable on that. What were you thinking?"

"That I'd sleep lightly and hear you if you needed me."

"Oh, Marshall." She straightened, tossing her hair over her shoulder as she did so. "You didn't even cover yourself with one of these throws and afghans around the room."

"They look too pretty to use. Besides, it was warm when I laid down. Even too warm to stay in my sweatshirt."

Yes, one of the first things she'd noticed was that he was half-naked. "I feel awful about this."

Stifling a groan as he sat up, he briskly rubbed his face. "Don't," he said, rising to his feet. "Remember, I'm a veteran of make-do sleeping quarters."

He was referring to the days, weeks and months in the hospital with Cynthia. That made Genevieve feel all the guiltier for adding to his discomfort. "Of course, but—you should have come to bed. There was plenty of room."

"I wouldn't have wanted to disturb you," he began. "I didn't think—" Pausing, he amended, "You wouldn't have minded?"

"Not at all. In fact, I think I was cold at one point and woke just enough to reach for the comforter. Your...body heat would have helped."

"How are you now?"

"Better. Fine, thanks to you. No queasiness whatsoever."

"Great. You look it. Fine."

He was noting her change in attire, and there was no missing that he more than approved of it. Aware that the stove light was probably exposing that she wasn't wearing a bra, she crossed her arms. Walking around without her robe was making her feel the night's chill and she didn't need to look down to know that her body was exposing that. As for her tunic—maybe it didn't cover her legs nearly as much as she thought. Staring at his chest helped. She didn't feel the coolness as much when she focused on something else—like the dusting of chest hair that didn't hide that his nipples were beading, as well.

"So, you've been here the whole time?" she asked as he reached for his shirt.

"You think I could leave you after you collapsed?" He hesitated then added, "I warned your mother that you might want her as backup if you woke and wanted me gone. I can call her if you wanted me to. She said she wouldn't mind whatever the time."

"Oh. No, don't do that." Genevieve couldn't believe she'd slept through phone conversations and everything. "She doesn't sleep well anywhere but at home."

"Then maybe we'll let her sleep. She did leave the decision up to me," he added.

Remembering some of her mother's comments about him, Genevieve felt heat rise in her face. "You have made a good impression on her."

"But less so on your neighbor."

She assumed that he was referring to the elderly couple she was sensitive about upsetting. "You met Riley? I assume it was Riley. Shirley rarely comes outside. She's on medication that discourages being in sunlight." Oh, blast, she thought. She was rambling. "Riley tends to come off as gruff, but he's really quite sweet. Hard of hearing, as you probably found out. And there are some dementia issues starting, as well."

"Which may explain why he has only one joke in his repertoire."

"Riley, not Rhett." Laughing breathlessly, Genevieve spontaneously reached out and touched his arm. "Poor Marshall. You got it from all sides today."

Looking from where her fingers rested back to her, he murmured, "It's all right. I'd do it again, and more... for you."

This was the Marshall Roark who for months had been creeping under her defenses and kept staking claim to bits of her heart. He stood with the shirt forgotten in his hands, his gaze willing her to take that necessary step closer. She understood that he was reluctant to this time. She'd rejected him too often for him to follow through on any impulses he might have. If she wanted him back, all that he was asking her to do was make the first move.

"Marshall," she breathed, shifting to lay her hand against his firmly beating heart. Lured by the entreaty in his eyes, as well as his male scent and body, she leaned forward to touch a kiss near where her fingers spanned.

Just as quietly, he dropped his shirt and slowly wrapped his arms around her. Being held against him with such tenderness made her feel safe. When he exhaled it sounded as if the night was also sighing with relief. She felt exactly the same way.

She closed her eyes, soaking in the sensations of him and this peace that she hadn't known in years and had only found again in his arms. His body was all male, as beautiful to the touch as to view, and as she skimmed her fingertips over his torso, she reveled at the power to make muscles harden and skin heat. With every caress, the cooler air became a relief for her own heating body.

As a content kitten would, she snuggled, rubbed her cheek against him, then wet him with the tip of her tongue. His taste made her yearn for more and she rose on tiptoe to seek his mouth.

With a moan he gave her what she asked for. He kissed her as if she was melting ice cream and he was starving and parched, dying of thirst. He only broke the kiss to breathe, and to journey down her throat and across the shoulder where her slipping nightshirt offered him more of her to explore. It was only when she took his hand and directed it to her breast that he broke their fragile silence.

"Genevieve. Are you sure you're up for this?"

"Not if we stand again."

"Oh, God, that was wonderful. You don't know how many times I've relived it in my mind. I can't stop think-ing about it."

He'd been stroking her from shoulder to hip and now slid both of his hands to her breasts, caressing her nipples with his thumbs until the hard peaks radiated an almost unbearable ache. She arched into his touch, praying he would never stop.

"I didn't get to do this enough that night," he said on shallow breaths. "I didn't get to learn the taste of every inch of you."

Nor she him. She stroked his shoulders, finding the increased tension there as lean muscle and tendons flexed and stretched under her touch. Then she returned to his front to lightly score his chest with her short fingernails.

She won a deeper moan from him as she learned how his nipples could make him ache just as he made hers.

"Wet me again. I promise I'll do that and more for you."

First she caressed him repeatedly with her nose and hair to sensitize him. By the time she grazed him with her teeth and closed her lips around him, his hands were moving more boldly under her tunic and inside her briefs to cup her bottom and rock her against his powerful arousal.

She'd noted before that he had the hands of a pianist. He used them with sensitivity and control, one moment exploring and coaxing, the next soothing and reassuring. Genevieve knew she would climax from his touch alone if he didn't enter her soon. Gliding her hand along the zipper of his jeans, she entreated, "Don't you want to lie down?"

"Soon."

First he slid his hands up her rib cage, lifting her tunic along the way. Seconds later it was over her head and gone. His caresses grew more decisive and passionate after that, his kisses damper until she had to cling to his shoulders to keep her balance.

"Lean back," he coaxed. "You know you're safe with me."

As he coursed a sensual river of hot caresses down her body she thought she would die from the exquisitely mellow, sometimes piercing pleasure. And still he continued, down her belly and over the waistband of her briefs, his breath hot between her thighs as he finished undressing her. She began to stop him from where he

was going. Only one man had ever touched her like that.
But he wouldn't let her. He wouldn't be denied.

By the time he lowered her onto the couch, she was
trembling and crying. Marshall rose over her and quickly
wrapped her in his arms.

"Genevieve, sweetheart, what's wrong?"

"It was so beautiful."

"You're what's beautiful."

"You make me ache."

"Ache bad or ache good?"

"I want you."

"Hold on."

His slow invasion was easier this time, yet still had
her arching her back and lifting her hips off the couch.
"Easy," he instructed, his voice almost a raw rasp. "We
have all night. Don't let me hurt you."

But she needed to be closer, needed him deeper.

Her eagerness was his undoing. When he started to
withdraw and she refused to let him, in fact wrapped
her legs around him to keep him close, he uttered a deep
growl and crushed her against him.

"You make me crazy," he said before locking his
mouth to hers. "Ah, Gen—"

Unable to stop, he drove back into her again and again.
Each thrust won a soft keen from her as she felt herself
driven back to where he'd already brought her once. The
pressure built. Droplets fell from his forehead and chest
as he struggled to prolong things. But as she greedily
licked at every drop to take everything he offered, she
also took the last of his control.

In his climax, she found her own, and as he fell onto
her in exhaustion, she clung to him, convinced that his

weight was the only thing to keep her from floating away in ecstasy.

At some point he moved them to make her more comfortable and they lay in each other's arms for a small eternity, panting yet continuing to stroke and calm each other. Genevieve might have drifted off to sleep, she was that content, but he began to speak.

"I think you're going to hate me by daylight. I kept trying not to rip you to shreds with this beard. You're too tempting for your own good."

When he began to withdraw, she immediately tightened her arms and legs to keep him close. "Please don't go."

"Sweetheart, you're not used to this."

"I loved your passion."

"You inspire me." As he teased her with a slow, gentle rocking of his hips, he added, "Truth is, I don't want to let go of you for fear that you'll escape."

"I won't go farther than my bed—if you'll take me there."

He lifted his head and searched her eyes. "Do you have an extra razor?"

"I just bought a new supply."

With a satisfied growl, he swept her into his arms and carried her to the bedroom.

When Marshall woke, his first reaction was a bursting feeling in his chest. Although he shifted his hand against his chest, he was fairly confident that he wasn't having a heart attack, but could a man die of too much happiness? Last night had tested that theory.

He hadn't quite gotten over the habit of wearing a

watch and, lifting his arm, he saw it was almost seven in the morning. They had been at each other so much through the night, he doubted they'd had three hours' sleep. At first he'd worried about the baby, but each time their lovemaking had been slower and more sensuous, unlike the impatient and desperate madness of their first union.

Genevieve. Just thinking her name made his eyes burn and throat ache with emotion. She'd been a dream, so generous, so responsive. If he'd had any doubts before— and there were virtually none—he knew he loved her. There was still much to learn about her, but the thought of spending the rest of their lives doing so filled him with a sense of rightness, as well as excitement.

He watched her shift onto her side, her movements cautious. Was she sore, or was she being thoughtful and trying not to wake him? As she reached out to check the clock, he was tempted to tease her by growling, "Get back here, woman." Her soft sound of surprise had him smiling anyway. He didn't remember the last time he'd slept so late either.

Something changed then. She stiffened and he watched as she eased up on one elbow. He could barely see what she was staring at but caught enough to realize it was a frame. That was when he remembered what else was on that bed stand. Adam's picture. In the midst of all their passion, they'd both forgotten that they'd been in the presence of that all night. He groaned inwardly and wanted her to turn away from it and make her reach for him. Instead, he watched in growing misery as she carefully turned it facedown on the night table.

And then, abruptly, she bounded out of bed and ran to the bathroom. Seconds later he heard her gagging.

Marshall winced for her misery. Morning sickness was bad enough, but to know she had suddenly gotten so upset from realizing all that had happened in the presence of that picture was more than he could bear. His heart had been so full of joy a moment ago; now he felt as if he was being eviscerated. Throwing aside the covers, he reached for his clothes.

By the time he was dressed, things had quieted in the bathroom. He made himself go to the door. "Genevieve—are you all right?"

"I'm sorry. Not really. I—I just need a little more time."

"I understand." Turning to look back at the face-down frame on the bed stand, he thought, *More than you know*.

He crossed the room and set the photo upright again. "You win," he murmured.

Genevieve didn't immediately think anything when she emerged from the shower and found Marshall gone. From her perspective, she couldn't imagine any man wanting to witness what she was going through, regardless of how pleased he was about a pregnancy. She figured he'd gone and used the main bathroom or was making coffee in the kitchen.

"I'm drying my hair," she called. "Join you in a few minutes. Could you make me a cup of instant decaf while you're brewing regular for yourself?"

When there was no reply, she still didn't think anything of it. It wasn't as if she needed it so badly that she expected him to bring her the coffee back here. She wasn't even sure her tummy could handle more than a sip or two.

Time-wise, she realized that she wasn't really running late. It was barely past eight o'clock now and although Ina was often at the office by 8:30, she, Avery and Raenne sometimes didn't arrive before 9:00 if it was a slow day.

That said, when she finally was dressed in a black knit pantsuit over a red short-sleeved sweater, she came out into the living room, then checked out the kitchen, and was startled to realize that the house was empty. In fact there was no sign that Marshall had ever been there.

She looked for a note and didn't find any. That sent her back to check the other shower, and she discovered that it hadn't been used. It was when she looked outside and saw no Mercedes that she accepted the truth. He must have left right after she'd told him she needed a little time. Had he misunderstood and thought she'd meant space?

Returning inside, she went back to her bedroom and viewed her messages on the BlackBerry. There were several, but his wasn't among them.

Despite taking a deep breath and warning herself not to panic, another wave of nausea struck her. Setting the device right in front of Adam's photo, she ran to the bathroom.

Her phone was playing Beethoven's Fifth when she next emerged. Not in the mood to deal with her mother, but resigned that she'd better or else Marshall wouldn't be able to get through if he wanted to, she keyed the button to take the call.

"Morning, Mother."

"How are you feeling, darling?"

"I thought I was fine the rest of yesterday and through the night, but almost as soon as I woke this morning, I was sick and ten minutes later I was sick again—and I haven't had so much as a sip of juice or water."

"Poor dear. I'd hoped you would be one of the lucky ones to escape that condition. Where's Marshall? Does he know?"

No way was she about to tell her that they'd spent the night together. But she didn't quite know what to say instead. "I don't know where he is," she said, trying to act casual. "That's fine. He's done enough. He needs his time and I certainly need mine." Her heart wrenched painfully as she heard herself speak such nonsense, but she wanted to make her mother quit talking about him. "At any rate, I'm heading to the office shortly." As soon as she applied another layer of foundation to try to hide the whisker burns. Marshall had shaved after bringing her to bed, but the number of abrasions on her body was testament to the intensity of their lovemaking beforehand.

"I can't see how that would be wise. At least wait a bit until you're sure the symptoms have definitely ceased. You'll have those women mad at you thinking you're exposing them to germs, and you won't be able to correct that without them putting two and two together. I've always believed our sex doesn't need a sixth sense in figuring out who's suffering from morning sickness."

"You're not helping, Mother."

"Well, if I'm not supposed to speak, do you want me to come over and run errands, clean?"

And see her stressing out as she waited for some

explanation from Marshall? Or falling apart if he didn't call? Or question her careful movements because of the love spots that had made it a small agony to put on a bra and panties this morning?

"No, not to worry. If things get any worse, we can discuss it."

"All right then. But call your doctor!"

"That goes without saying."

"And let me hear from you when you know something."

"I should be in touch by noon."

As he tossed his suitcase onto the bed, Marshall's gaze was drawn to the BlackBerry a foot away where he'd flung it earlier. He willed it to ring, but that didn't happen.

No, he couldn't do it. Genevieve had been clear—she wanted to be left alone. When she was ready to speak to him, she would let him know. In the meantime, he needed to do something and driving was a good start. He had no idea where he planned to go; he just knew he couldn't stay here in this house where he'd first held her and made love to her. He would finish losing what was left of his sanity if he did.

When the house phone began ringing, he frowned. Having been his real estate agent first, Genevieve had gotten into the habit of calling his BlackBerry instead of the house number. But on the chance that his assumption was incorrect, he grabbed the remote before the answering machine was triggered.

"Roark."

"What's wrong?" Sydney demanded.

Marshall was surprised at her agitation, but wary, too. "Nothing that I know of," he said evasively. "Why?"

"I just called Genevieve and she's planning to go to the office. Why aren't you talking her out of it? For that matter, why are you at home? You said you'd watch over her. You can't let her keep taking such risks with her health."

"She must be feeling that she can manage that," he said.

"You don't know? You two haven't talked? She says she didn't know where you were."

She knew; he suspected that she just didn't want to tell her mother what happened last night any more than he intended to. "I was going to check on her after a while." At some point he needed to let Genevieve know that she could still reach him if need be—although he doubted that was likely to happen.

"Did you two have a quarrel?" Sydney countered. "She said that you needed your space and she needed hers."

Marshall all but dropped the phone. She'd said *that?* Only minutes ago? Things were even worse than he expected if she'd exposed that much to her mother, who didn't seem to be able to keep a confidence to save her life. "No. No quarrel." He could barely get those words out.

"You didn't pressure her again, did you? Forgive me for venturing into personal territory, but she is my daughter. She told me that you had a tendency to be controlling. She quickly excused you, of course. She said it was a residual effect of having been Cynthia's caretaker for so long. I hope that's all it is and not something deeper-seated."

Marshall's insides roiled, even as he reminded himself that a daughter had a right to speak to her mother, particularly when she was the only family there was available to discuss things with. But that didn't mean he had to.

"Sydney, I really don't feel comfortable talking about my relationship with Genevieve with you. Just know that the matter has been discussed and leave it at that. All I care about is her health and happiness."

"We both do, that's why I'm calling. I really am on your side, Marshall, leery though I am of rebound marriages. On the other hand, I'm walking proof that they work, aren't I?"

Her girlish giggle grated and had him all the more anxious to get off the phone. "Yes, you are," he said politely, keeping his skepticism to himself. "And thanks for the vote of confidence. Now I need to finish packing."

"Packing?"

"A business matter has come up." It was the first thing to pop into his mind.

"How long will you be gone?"

"I'm not sure. Probably not more than a few days." He figured his new security system was competent, but it wouldn't hurt for her to know that he wouldn't be around. Sydney Sawyer was undoubtedly better than a watchdog and equal to his house's alarm system.

"I see. Does Genevieve know this?"

"I...only just found out myself." Pacing, he rubbed at his forehead, trying to keep his impatience from entering his voice. "I intend to call her as soon as I finish packing."

"Oh, good. Well, then have a safe trip, dear. I'll watch for your return."

Disconnecting, Marshall muttered, "I'll bet you will."

He hadn't intended to try calling Genevieve until he was on the road, but under the circumstances, he keyed her number within seconds. He didn't need her mother beating him to it—and adding her twenty cents.

"Marshall," Genevieve said upon immediately answering. "I'm glad you called. I'm sorry—I mean, I obviously upset you."

"Well, it was pretty clear you were embarrassed, although there was no need to be. But I respected that you wanted some space." He used those words specifically hoping she understood that he knew about her chat with her mother.

After a slight hesitation, she replied, "I am having more trouble adjusting to this condition than I expected I would."

With her condition *and* with being his lover, he thought, feeling as though he was bleeding internally. As painful as that truth was, he still cared too much to make things more difficult for her. Rubbing at his forehead, he said, "Maybe when I get back, you'll have some answers."

"You're going somewhere?"

"Yes, a business matter has come up. It can't be helped. It should only take a few days, but—look, you have my number. If you want—if you need anything, you know how to get hold of me."

She didn't answer right away and he knew she was waiting for him to explain said business. He didn't dare try because he didn't have a clue.

"Did we get disconnected?" he asked instead.

"No, it's…oh, this horrible condition. I needed a second to let it pass. Okay then…I'll see you when you get back?"

Where was the "Don't go!" entreaty he was desperate to hear? He'd become addicted to hearing her say it last night as in, "Don't stop," "Don't let me go." He could even survive with a bland, "I'll miss you."

"Yes," he replied gruffly. "Take care of yourself, Genevieve. Keep that doctor's number handy."

"Actually, we talked minutes ago," she replied. "I'm going in today. The near fainting spell worried her and she's determined to fit me in."

"That's good. Excellent." That was at least one bit of good news. "Will you let me know if she voices a concern about anything?"

"I never forget that this is your baby, too. I just didn't know if you'd mind since you'll be busy and all."

What he minded was that they were talking as though last night hadn't happened—or more accurately, that it was the biggest mistake of her life. "Call," he rasped. Then he disconnected because it hurt too damned much to listen to any more.

In the end, Genevieve bought herself more time from the eagle-eyed trio at the office and never bothered going in. Her appointment was for ten o'clock and she gauged it would take a half hour to get to the clinic. Besides, after her conversation with Marshall, she didn't yet trust her emotions and could use the extra time to pull herself together. She called Ina and told her that she would see them after lunch. Ina was sympathetic but relieved to hear of the appointment. Genevieve let her continue believing that she was seeing her regular doctor. Considering Marshall's abrupt departure from town, there was now even less of a rush than before to disclose her true condition.

What she hadn't anticipated was to start getting weepy every few minutes. She hadn't been so bad since she'd suffered the blow of Adam's loss. As if the morning sickness wasn't punishment enough. But her heart was aching from the remoteness she'd heard in Marshall's voice. What had happened to the man who couldn't stop touching her last night? Was the business trip even real? Surely he didn't have to do such a convoluted thing to show her that he wanted to put some distance between them?

Could it be that with Cynthia's suffering still fresh in his memory, her condition had become too much for him? He had to know that it was temporary?

As a new wave of nausea assaulted her and she rushed for the bathroom, she thought, *Please, God...let it be temporary.*

Although Dr. Tracy Nyland explained that she wouldn't be able tell anything regarding her blood and urine tests until the results came back from the lab in a few days, Genevieve underwent a full exam and was deemed in good shape...with conditions. From the answers to her questions, Dr. Nyland did suspect she was slightly anemic and prescribed vitamins. She also listened to Genevieve's rendition of her usual workweek, and recommended she start reducing her hours closer to fifty rather than seventy-five. She explained that alone should reduce some of the stress.

"Given the tragic loss of your late husband," the soft-spoken brunette said, her gray eyes warm with compassion, "I totally understand why you would have focused all of your energy on your career. However, your baby deserves a mother who's not only physically able to nurture it, but one who is psychologically and emotionally willing to do that, as well."

Genevieve experienced a pang of guilt. Hadn't Marshall said virtually the same thing? Yet she had seen his concern for her as possessiveness. He'd wanted more of her time and attention for himself. All he'd been doing was trying to protect her from bad habits acquired over years of grief.

"You've heard it before, but it's a rule of thumb full of wisdom," Tracy Nyland continued. "'Everything in moderation.'"

When she finished writing her prescriptions, the doctor leaned forward over her clasped hands and smiled warmly across her desk at Genevieve. "Now you told me there are some complications with the father. I don't mean to embarrass you, but from the intimacy signs on your body, it looks like you two share a healthy relationship."

It was all Genevieve could do not to writhe, she was so mortified. She'd totally forgotten that Dr. Nyland would see the effects of last night, too, until she'd been on the examination table. It got a little less humiliating when the woman urged her, "Call me Tracy. Let's talk woman to woman."

"We seem to be running hot and cold," Genevieve replied. "He claims to be ecstatic about the baby, but today he's left for a business trip to I don't know where."

"Could it be that you've been giving him those same hot-cold signals?" Tracy asked. "There's no set timeline on grieving, and part of your morning sickness problem may be psychosomatic. You said you suffered a great deal of nausea after your late husband died. You know in some cultures there's a belief that something like your chronic nausea and vomiting is your inner core's rejection of what life is handing you. You couldn't bear Adam's loss, so you rejected it. Or put it this way, you ejected what was unacceptable to you. Now you find yourself pregnant during an extremely inopportune time and the father is someone you have strong feelings for, but you're rejecting the idea that you could love again. Maybe love as you deeply as you did before."

Genevieve went all but slack-jawed. "You're telling me that I'm *making* myself throw up?"

"I've no doubt that your body chemistry is involved, but you could be helping things along," Nyland replied. "I'll give you a list of a few book titles you might want to look into. You don't have to buy into the whole philosophy—I certainly don't—but I suspect you'll find some of it helpful and fascinating."

Later, as she sat in her SUV, Genevieve reported the doctor's recommendations to her mother. "I should be much improved by Thanksgiving. She recommended I try to avoid strong perfumes, too."

"How are you going to do that?" her mother asked with no small disdain. "Give up breathing around Avery?"

Genevieve ignored the sarcasm, especially since she thought Avery's scent was intriguing and right for her. "She said the same about foods that are strongly aromatic. Oh, and to try cool rather than hot meals, and that some women had good results with adding higher protein to their diets."

"I could have told you that much," her mother replied. "I must have consumed an entire side of beef by myself when I carried you. I barely had a bout of the morning horror."

"Mother, please." No way would Genevieve tell her about Tracy's more unorthodox ideas about her stomach problems.

"Sorry. I'm glad you went, darling. Did you let Marshall know?"

"I'll probably wait until I get the test results next week—or when he returns if there's nothing out of the norm."

Sydney's indelicate response was followed by, "What I'd like to know is why he didn't postpone his trip and go with you?"

"It's not like an ultrasound or anything. Besides, he had business out of town."

"Doesn't that make you wonder? He sold his businesses. One of the things that was getting to you was that he had nothing *but* time on his hands and was fixating on you."

That was then. Now that she thought she understood him better and trusted her heart, she yearned for his company. This abrupt departure was really throwing her.

"It could be something connected to Cynthia's estate. Stop speculating." Genevieve felt a lump growing in her throat. But if she sobbed while on the phone with her mother, there was no telling what Sydney Sawyer would do. "I have to get back to the office, and I still need to stop and pick up the vitamins Dr. Nyland recommended. Talk later." She hung up.

"Oh, God," she whispered as she started down the road. On this occasion, she had to agree with her mother: she didn't believe Marshall's "business trip" excuse, either. "What happened? Why did you really leave, Marshall?"

When she got home from the office that evening, she didn't feel better emotionally, but her physical symptoms had eased—possibly due to Avery and her exotic perfume being absent. She'd also eaten lightly and with care. Nevertheless, her heart was growing heavier with every passing hour.

Unable to settle down, she paced through her house, an old habit when she couldn't sleep, but thinking gave her no answers. She paused where Marshall had slept and leaned over to catch his scent on the cushions. She found it again on her bed and curled there hoping for the oblivion of sleep, but didn't find that relief, either.

She checked her BlackBerry frequently. The only message was a reminder about choir practice the next night, which she already knew she wouldn't be attending. In fact, she wondered how long it would be before she was asked not to participate any longer. Somehow that bothered her less today than it would have yesterday.

The tears started again. Hoping to stem them, she

went back to pacing through the house while doing some deep-breathing exercises. It eventually came to her that she was trying to avoid the photos spread around the house. Finally, inevitably, she stopped at the one in the living room. For quite some time it had been soothing to have it and the others to talk to and to keep Adam's handsome face fresh in her mind. But in another moment of clarity, she realized that the full reason she'd turned the picture in her bedroom facedown that morning was because she was accepting that things did have to change. She could no longer come to these singular shrines throughout her house. She couldn't use him to work through her problems, or lie in bed at night and share events of the day, and her deepest thoughts. She couldn't make him her means to escape dealing with her own life issues, either. He was gone and that would always weigh heavily in her heart, but she had been left to keep living. And living meant to open herself and her heart to the new experiences life brought her—like love.

One by one, she collected the photographs and brought them to her office. She'd gone into a storage box in the utility closet and retrieved her supply of Christmas tissue paper. Almost with the same painstaking care that she'd first framed them, she ceremoniously and lovingly closed them away in the box.

There was no box to resolve her dilemma about Marshall.

On the first Monday in October, she received the news from Dr. Nyland that her tests had come back confirming that she was in excellent health and that if all continued well, they could do an ultrasound just before Thanksgiving. That gave her a little boost until the thought came like a black cloud—what if Marshall was no longer in her life then?

That made her decide to bring Ina, Avery and Raenne into the loop, situation-wise. They were driving her crazy anyway. She knew she was acting more subdued, despite some relief from the morning sickness. And she was crediting that to giving more attention to what and how she ate, not the fact that she was moving on with her past. However, they were the ones who kept noting that her phones were quieter, and Avery point-blank asked her what she'd done to Marshall that he hadn't shown his "brooding poet's" face lately, either. They knew something was up despite her brief explanation that he was out of town on business.

But as plans often go, later that afternoon, just when she was deciding that she might as well admit that she was pregnant, so they would know to help her monitor the stages of her pregnancy, Beethoven's Fifth chimed on her BlackBerry, putting that meeting on hold.

"He's home!" her mother declared.

Weak-kneed, Genevieve sank into her office chair and almost started to hyperventilate. She pressed her hand to her heart. "When?"

"I think just now. Bart and I were in Texarkana all day, so we're only now getting back. The garage door was closing behind his Mercedes. I don't think he saw us. Has he called you yet?"

"No." Then she added with false reassurance, "But I'm sure he will. He'll need to turn off the alarm and check the house first."

"I'm sure." However, Sydney didn't sound at all convinced, or happy to know she'd been the one to have to pass on the news. "I've a good mind to go over there right this minute and give him a good talking-to."

Her mother had called at least twice a day, her first question always being, "Have you heard from him?" Now Genevieve had to admonish her. "Stay out of it, Mother."

"He's breaking your heart."

"I have always stayed out of your relationship with Bart, haven't I? Even when you scared me to death picking him up so quickly after your divorce."

"I did not *pick him up*. He approached me."

"After you spotted him—that's the story you've always confessed to once you have two martinis in you."

"Oh, I miss those things," Sydney lamented. "They give me dreadful headaches though. Well, seeing that no good deed goes unpunished, I'm going to go have a glass of wine with Bart and listen to him explain our Houston itinerary for the sixth time."

About to beg her mother to think of her husband a little more instead of feeling sorry for herself, she bit her tongue. "Give him a hug from me," she said instead.

As brave and bold as she had been with her mother, Genevieve quickly lost all confidence when the minutes dragged on and an hour later there was no call from Marshall. It was closing in on five o'clock when, unable to bear sitting there pretending to see anything on her computer screen, she snatched up her things and left, telling a startled Ina that she needed to go home.

Riley Butler was shuffling the long haul to the mailbox as she turned into her driveway. Shifting into Park,

Genevieve got out of the SUV and went to say hello to him. It had been several days since they'd talked and she was usually better with checking on him and his wife.

"It's good to see you taking advantage of this gorgeous weather," she began as she drew nearer. When she reached him, she gave him a big hug and peck on the cheek.

"Do that again. Maybe Shirl will look out the window and get a little jealous. An old buzzard like me needs all the help he can get."

Genevieve happily complied, enjoying his laughter at his own humor more. "How are you holding up?"

"Not worth a .22 short," he said as usual.

Thank goodness Riley's son, Raymond, had taken the former hunter's shooting arms away from him. Although Genevieve knew Riley was kidding her now, she wasn't so sure he would be if something happened to his precious Shirley, whose inquiries into her welfare were equally repetitious: "Sometimes so—sometimes so."

Genevieve gazed around the Butlers' yard with its Secret Garden clutter of plants and yard ornaments and said, "You still have the best color regardless of the season."

"Gonna depend on the cardinals, blue jays and finches to provide that pretty soon, I expect. Don't think I have the energy to keep up with things the way I used to."

She made a mental note to bring them at least two poinsettias for their larger front and back windows and a bag of narcissus bulbs and potting soil so Riley could have indoor blooms to carry him and his Shirley through the winter and past the spring frosts. Their son, Raymond, was pretty good about visiting but lived and worked in the DFW area. That and three growing kids claimed most of his thoughts as much as his income. He probably wouldn't think of little things that fed the soul of the elderly.

"Is Shirl still crocheting?"

"Pancakes."

"I think she calls them pot holders, Riley."

"Silly things are the size of flapjacks as my gramps used to call 'em."

"I hope she saves me a pair," Genevieve said. "I've about worn out the last set she gave me."

The old man cast her a tender look. "Bless you. You know full well you have enough of those things to carpet your living room." He looked at the sky and lifted his collar around his scrawny neck. "Wind is picking up. Front is gonna make us old-timers with chronic hurts miserable tonight. Stay warm, angel."

With her eyes burning from repressed tears, Genevieve returned to her car and drove it into her garage. She didn't know how she would bear it if she lost one or both of the Butlers on top of Marshall this year.

Riley was right—a colder-than-usual front was approaching. It was time to add a blanket to the bed, especially since she slept alone and there was no help to help keep things warm. "Maybe I'll get a dog," she said to herself. That would supply some body heat.

But she knew her timing was off. She was trying to add hours into her day, not subtract them. And having a newborn was the world's worst time to train a new pet.

She did, though, make a mental note to transition the thermostat from cool to heat, and to check the pilot on the furnace and change the air filter. She wouldn't need a serviceman for any of that, but the loneliness that came with the idea of watching seasons—and the holidays—come and go by herself for yet another year dealt her another debilitating blow.

She had changed into a soft velour pajama/lounge set in a powder blue and was trying to convince herself to take out something from the freezer to nuke in the microwave when the doorbell rang. Since it was still daylight—barely—and she didn't put it past Riley to have grabbed a handful of Shirl's pot holders to bring over, she opened the door without hesitation. To her amazement, Marshall stood there instead.

Her first thought was, *He didn't use his key.*

He was wearing a deep-blue sports jacket that matched his eyes, jeans and a gray crew-necked sweater and held the largest bouquet of white and red roses that she'd ever seen. But more memorable was the look on his face. She'd never seen so many emotions play on his face at one time before.

"Look who's back in town," he said.

Not knowing what to say in reply, Genevieve stepped aside to let him in. She wasn't so confident about shutting the door behind him, but the fact that he was here merited something.

She accepted the bouquet with a murmured, "Thank you," but the ache in the vicinity of her heart kept her from being able to smile. "It looks like you hit every florist in town." There were four in total.

"Just about. The idea was to impress, not to wrench your back from the weight or stab you to death with the thorns."

His corny humor almost succeeded in tugging at the

corners of her mouth. What helped was thinking that this might explain why it took so long for him to get here. "Have you been back long?"

"You know how long I've been back."

Advantage, Sydney, she thought, but she only shrugged to Marshall. "When I didn't hear from you day after day and through the weekend, I started to think I never would."

"I was trying to give you the space you wanted—or make you miss me."

Something nagged at her memory, but she shook her head at his reasoning. "When you left so abruptly, you hurt me."

This time he indicated his confusion, his sweeping arm gesture looking more like a broken wing. "You made it clear that you wanted me to."

"What are you talking about? After experiencing one of the most amazing nights of my life, you vanished without a note or anything. The next thing I knew you had to leave on a business trip when you hadn't mentioned business in all the time we'd been together, except for the ones you sold."

"That started because of your mother. I had to tell her something to get her off the phone. She called as I was first packing and—"

"There! You see—you intended to leave even before talking to her."

"You wanted me to."

Genevieve's hold on the roses threatened to make them keel over in her grip. But if thorns were stabbing her, she didn't feel a thing. "Why do you keep saying that? We made love all night long. Then my morning sickness came back with a vengeance."

"No, you woke and the first thing you did was look at Adam's picture. I could tell you were so ashamed over what, to me, was the night of my life. You turned the photo facedown as though you couldn't bear to deal with the guilt of what we'd shared." Marshall swallowed. "I'm not jealous of a dead man. Okay, scratch that. But I could understand how much you loved and missed him. This... It was seeing that you were sorry for what happened between us that was too much. I needed time to come to terms with the fact that I'll always be second to him." Slowly, carefully, he took hold of her arms. "The fact remains—you're having my baby. Mine. And I love you. I've proven that I can make you want me, and I know you like me...at least when I'm not being a controlling jerk." He released her only to reach into his jacket pocket and take out a small jewelry box. "If you give me the chance, one day I could make you love me back."

Genevieve looked from the black velvet box to him and her eyes started to fill. "You don't know anything," she said, her voice shaking.

He blinked.

"I looked at the photo, yes, and put it down, yes. I was saying goodbye." She gestured to the room. "Look around. They're all gone. After our night together, I realized it was time. To be with *you,* I had to let him go."

Marshall didn't look. He didn't take his eyes off her except to close them for a moment and swallow again. Harder this time. When he opened his eyes, a bright smile lit his face that rivaled a sky full of rockets. "You love me?"

"Yes, and missing you was making me sicker than the morning sickness does." When he stepped forward to sweep her into his arms, she cried, "Wait!"

Chapter Eight

"Let me borrow your jacket for a second," Genevieve told him.

Although perplexed, Marshall removed it and held it for her as she slipped it on, then he watching in disbelief as she pulled a white and red rose from the bouquet. Shoving them at him, she said, "Hold these a minute."

Incredulous, he watched her run next door and knock, then call inside to her neighbors, the Butlers. As adorable as she looked swallowed up in his clothing, to him it took longer than potholes to be filled before old Riley opened up. The man shouted in delight and accepted the roses and her hug.

By the time she returned, Marshall had the two remaining roses in a bud vase he'd located in a kitchen cabinet. Once she locked up and met him breathless but grinning in the kitchen, he snatched up the black box from the counter, pretending that he suspected she was about to take off with it, too.

"Absolutely not. Gifting the roses was touching, but you are not giving this away."

He pretty much failed at his debut in acting. He couldn't come close to mimicking "stern" when he was finally able to breathe again without feeling as if a razor was turning his insides into mincemeat.

"No," Genevieve said, stepping into his arms. "That and you, I would very much like to keep."

At last, he thought as he drew her against him. It was true. The photos were gone. She wanted a life with him. He'd driven close to a thousand circuitous miles, sat for countless hours trying to think of a way to brainwash, bribe and even blackmail her into marrying him, but just now she'd given him her heart without ever opening the box he had brought her.

He kissed her because he had no words that could surpass showing her what that meant and what he felt. He'd missed her so badly, he fully expected to end up in E.R. somewhere from some kind of hemorrhage. But as she kissed him back, the healing began.

"Don't ever go away like that again," she entreated, gasping for breath.

"Never."

"I missed you so."

"Believe me, I missed you more."

She pressed her cheek against his shoulder. "Where did you go?"

"Around. All over East Texas." He had missed this goddess hair, the way she instinctively curved into him as though whatever part of them wasn't touching left her bereft. "While I was trying to figure out how to win your heart, I figured I might as well look for a boat."

"A boat…that was your business trip?"

"Love, you know there was no business trip. As I began driving, I thought about that boathouse and dock and figured there should be a boat."

"You've traveled back and forth from Dallas for how long, most of the time driving by Lake Ray Hubbard, and you didn't figure out there are plenty of boat dealers within an hour of here?"

"Yes, and one of them is delivering my choice next week." Marshall didn't want to talk about that. He couldn't believe that she wasn't grabbing for the box. "Aren't you even interested in seeing this ring?"

"Marshall, if you like it, I know I will, too."

This woman, he thought. He knew she would forever mystify yet enchant him.

"I have a story," he began. "Sydney will love this."

"Leave Sydney out of it."

"I happened upon an estate sale," he said, determined to get it said. "There was a story to *that,* but it can wait. Suffice it to say I spotted a ring that was handed down for generations, but now there were no heirs. The last woman who wore it was one of the first prominent real estate brokers in the region. That and its elegance convinced me that it was the perfect ring for you." He released her only to open the box.

Genevieve gasped. "Oh, it's beautiful!"

And fit perfectly, Marshall thought with no small satisfaction. Somehow he knew it would.

The ring was a three-carat square diamond surrounded by twelve smaller diamonds set in platinum. Admiring the way it sparkled as it reflected the kitchen lights, she said, "Marshall, it's too much."

"No, it's nothing less than you deserve." He lifted her hand to his lips. "Whatever vows we take before others, this is for your ears alone. Genevieve Marie Gale…I've never loved like this. I know with a certainty, I never will again."

Genevieve caressed his cheek. "You were so unexpected. I thought this wasn't possible."

It thrilled him to hear her confession, particularly after her resistance to him and those painful denials. Those memories would fade quickly and he knew exactly how he wanted to help obliterate them.

"Make love with me," he said, easing the jacket off her and drawing her into his arms again. While it wasn't that chilly outside yet, he had soon understood, and had already seen, why she'd needed to cover up—she wasn't wearing anything beneath that top. He couldn't wait any longer to remove it, too.

"Yes," she whispered.

As she wrapped her arms around his neck, he lifted her into his arms and carried her to her bedroom. With the closed blinds and heavy drapes, the room was almost dark, but he could see her serene smile. The night-light in the bathroom lit golden lights in her eyes that outsparkled her ring. Her hair shimmered like spun silk. He stroked it before cupping her face within his hands and kissing her with aching tenderness.

They undressed each other with the same care and leisure, lingering to worship and explore. There was all the time in the world now. What was more, he loved the creamy smoothness of her skin and the way it warmed under his hands and mouth. Before the night was over, he wanted to make her burn for him. But slow and thorough was already enough for him to heat to fever pitch for her. Of course, her touch had a part in that. If he'd needed reassurance of her adoration, she proved it with every sweep of her fingers and caress of her lips.

When they were finally in bed, even though he was hard and aching to be inside her, he started his exploration and worship all over again because he loved hearing her soft sighs of pleasure, tiny whimpers of hunger, and the way she stretched, arched and pressed closer to get everything that he offered. It was when he lingered on her breasts that she actually trembled.

"It should be impossible for you to get any more sensitive there," he murmured, inciting, then soothing with his mouth.

"I'll never be able to wear an unpadded bra again," she confessed. "All I have to do is think of you and anyone with eyes can tell what's happening to me."

"And what happens when I look at you?" he teased, sliding his hand between her thighs.

A brief whimper broke past her lips. "You know."

"I know…and that's going to make it damned near impossible to walk around in public. Jeez, you're small there. How on earth are you going to deliver a baby?"

"The same way I can accept you," she said, a smile in her voice.

Rising above her, he felt his hard length seek and find her warm and moist center. "Then we'd better practice a lot of stretching."

Marshall groaned as he eased into her. He knew he could climax in two strokes; it seemed a month since that night they'd shared. To delay that, he thought of the beginning at his house. "Confess—I hurt you our first time?"

"You soon made me forget it."

"Did I?"

She tightened her muscles around him. "Yes."

Sucking in a sharp breath, he thrust deeper. "What can I do for you now?"

"Just don't stop," she said, her voice growing thinner.

Ah, he thought. He had come full circle.

The playfulness ending, Marshall kissed her, claiming her mouth as he did her body and, cupping her hips, he led them both to a place that was theirs alone. The tighter she wrapped herself around him, the more forceful his thrusts became.

"I love you," he rasped, feeling the end coming. And before she could reply, he locked his mouth to hers again, claiming her cry of ecstasy just as she consumed his.

It was almost midnight when Genevieve lay with her head on Marshall's chest, her ring brilliant against the dark hair there. They had dozed after their first reunion and had just made love again. Replete for the moment, she couldn't help but smile.

"What?"

It filled her with wonder that he was already so sensitive to her smallest reactions. "I was thinking about what you were like in high school and college. I'll bet you had girls flirting with you from every side and making it hard for you to study."

"You'd be wrong," he replied, stroking her hair. "I

was a serious kid, more worried about disappointing my father with my grades than collecting a harem like some of the sports jocks. My father was a corporate banker and felt I had the same acumen. As an only child, it was always expected that I would follow in his footsteps. He nearly disowned me when I got interested in the restaurant business."

"Did he come around eventually? You did well with them and your commercial real estate holdings."

"Some of his abilities couldn't help but rub off, I guess, considering that he bombarded me with enough lectures and lessons. But not well enough to play in the high-stakes games—and that's fine with me. I like to sleep at night."

"I knew you didn't have any siblings," Genevieve said, "but I didn't realize that about your father. You wanted a dad and you got a CEO for a parent. Is he still alive?"

"No, my father died three years ago. My mother last year."

Genevieve shifted onto her tummy to gaze at him. "I'm sorry. With Cynthia being so ill, that must have been an enormously stressful time for you."

"It gave me some strong insights into who and what I didn't want to be." He shifted so he could press his ear to her tummy. "Still pretty quiet in there." When he raised his head, his expression was beseeching. "If my hunch is right and we have a son, please don't ask for us to make him a junior? Marshall was my father's middle name— Edmund Marshall Roark, and I don't want our son to be saddled with unnecessary pressure and expectaions."

It took Genevieve several seconds to recover from

the spasm of pain she felt for the lonely boy he'd been. "What did you have in mind?"

"The name of an old teacher of mine. He was everything I thought a parent should be. He passed away last year. His name was Robert."

"Robert Roark. I like it. And if it's a girl?"

He gave her an apologetic smile. "Sweetheart, the Roarks tend to produce males." Caressing her swollen lower lip with his thumb, he said, "Are you going to run screaming from this bed if I confess that I was serious about having another child someday? Preferably three. If this delivery is too difficult, we could look into adoption."

This revelation and emotional hunger touched Genevieve deeply. "You *are* serious about wanting to be a family man." She loved that realization just as she adored him for being so concerned about her ability to deliver a child safely. "Really, Marshall, regardless of my parents' inability to conceive after me or what you incorrectly see as a lacking in my build—"

"Darling, your body is exquisite," he said, running his hand over her bottom, then easily settling her between his thighs. "I'm trying to ensure that it's around for several more decades. Genevieve, the idea of you suffering when it's not entirely necessary—"

"But I'm beginning to like the idea of challenging you to add on rooms to this property without taking from the children's play areas."

Once he caught on, he grinned. "Is that revenge for jumping ahead of things and drafting plans for you to work from home more?"

Genevieve chuckled. "It might be the last chance I get

considering how busy you plan to keep me." Feeling him stir against her abdomen, she sat up and straddled him.

Narrowing his eyes, his mouth curving with appreciation, Marshall ran his hands up her sleek thighs and gripped her hips. But rather than settling her where he wanted her, he murmured, "You are so beautiful," and drew her back to his side. "We can't, darling. You have to be sore. At the very least, the baby is getting seasick."

Although she laughed softly, she had to admit she was a little tender. But that didn't stop her from wanting to touch and be touched by him. She reached below the blankets to caress him, drawing a short hiss.

"Genevieve, haven't you figured out yet that my will's not that strong where you're concerned?"

"Same here. So let me enjoy myself. Besides, my conscience is kicking in for giving away most of your flowers," she added, kissing her way down his chest. "I'm deeply sorry," she crooned, then with her tongue she circled his navel, and slid downward. "Deeply... deeply."

And then there were no words, just a woman welcoming her soul mate home and a weary but hopeful man grateful to have found his way back to her.

The next morning as Marshall considerately went off to make himself something to eat in Genevieve's kitchen to save her too many aromas, she dealt with her disruptive tummy and dressed. To her relief, as unwelcome as the nausea continued to be, it was a fraction as bad as on previous days.

By the time she joined him, he had ingested his omelet and managed to vent most of the food aroma from the house. What was more, he had set a place for her with a cup of yogurt and dry toast. Those two roses in the bud vase magically had moved from her nightstand to sit at the corner of her placemat.

Planting a kiss over her bemused smile, he said, "That's soy yogurt. It's even more soothing for your tummy and the toast is whole grain."

"How do you know about soy yogurt? More important, where did it come from?"

"Answer to question one—I have a computer and lots of time on my hands. Answer to question two—I have a car and used it while you were indelicately indisposed. Sit." He added a nuzzle to the side of her neck and murmured in appreciation. "I swear you smell and taste so good, I could have gobbled you up with my omelet."

Genevieve watched him circle back to the coffeemaker with his mug. She didn't know what she had done to deserve such a blessing twice in one lifetime. "I guess it's going to take me a little while to convince myself that this is happening. Women think most men would run in front of a bus to escape the side effects of a pregnancy. You try to soothe my morning sickness by finding something that will stay in my stomach."

Glancing over his shoulder, Marshall winked at her. "Darling, the dividends are mind-blowing. After last night, you couldn't run me off with a hamper full of timber rattlesnakes. So what's your schedule look like for today?"

"Pretty flexible until three in the afternoon when I'm showing a couple two properties."

He refilled his mug and brought it back to the table.

"Then what do you say we check and see if Sydney and Bart are available for a visit from us?"

Understanding his intent, she frowned while breaking off a corner of the toast. "I've a good mind to tell several people before I do her. Her speaking out of turn and interference overall caused you terrible pain."

"But her advice hit home. And it all worked out in the end, didn't it?" At her dubious look, he shrugged. "I'm feeling benevolent. If I can, will you?"

She supposed she could. But with no more enjoyment than she ate the toast. She thought she could get out of that by distracting him.

"I liked our reunion part," she said, glancing at him from beneath her lashes.

His eyes lit with humor. "I think we should reenact my return to Lake Starling at least once a month."

"Holding out on me, Mr. Roark? I thought it could become our Friday night tradition."

Marshall had to shift in his chair to a more comfortable position. "I like the way you think."

Growing more serious, Genevieve said, "If you don't mind, I'm going to tell the girls at the office before we go to Mother and Bart's. Could I interest you in coming along?"

"Absolutely. After all, I'm about to become a fixture around the place." Seeing that she had yet to taste her yogurt, Marshall took the spoon, scooped a bit from the cup and directed it to her mouth. "Open."

She did, but she wasn't all that gracious about it. Shuddering away the last effects, she asked, "What do you mean? You want to sell real estate here?"

"No, I want to get your building painted for you. It

looks like every one of your offices could use a fresh coat or two."

She stroked his arm with renewed appreciation. "My hero. I keep meaning to address that, but it usually stays on the bottom of the to-do list. That would be wonderful, thank you." This time she anticipated the next scoop of creamy yogurt like a baby bird spotting a parent with grubs and worms.

"You know my ulterior motive, don't you? That gives me the excuse to keep a closer eye on you and Baby."

"I never doubted it." The second spoonful of yogurt was no better than the first and she had to refuse any more. "Baby is saying 'yes' to toast and 'no' to yogurt."

Clearly in an amicable mood, Marshall put down the spoon. "What else would you like done there?"

"Nothing that I know of—yet. You can start over on your ideas about updating this place, though."

He took the hand closest to him and kissed it. "Thank you, my love."

"And I was thinking that the sooner I moved into your house—"

"Our house."

"—the easier it would be for contractors to work."

Keeping her smaller hand within both of his, Marshall nodded. "I haven't done anything with those boxes in my garage yet. I'll start transferring them here in the next few days."

"It's going to be difficult to tell Riley and Shirl. They're such sweet souls. They'll be heartbroken to see me leave."

"They won't be losing a friend and cherished

neighbor," he assured her. "They'll be gaining someone else who cares and will be there for them."

Genevieve's eyes threatened to flood. "My cup runneth over," she whispered.

"No tears, love. Change of subject."

She laughed and blinked away the tears. "One of us is going to get whiplash. Shoot."

"Do you want a big church wedding?"

That one was the easiest to answer. "Heavens, no. That's way too much work, a waste of money… Besides, we'll be busy enough doing everything you said, plus getting the nursery ready."

The word *nursery* won her an ardent and intimate look from him. "Let's elope to Vegas tonight."

"Too flashy and impersonal." She covered her flat tummy with both hands. "Besides, you're not getting me on a plane with this precious cargo."

"Good thought." He grew thoughtful. "We could have your minister or a judge come to the house. Either of the houses."

"I like that idea. But since this place is likely to have a 'For Sale' sign in front of it shortly, let's say your place?"

"*Our* place," he amended with a look.

Feeling impish, she replied, "Good, then it's settled—the lake house."

"Wise guy. Just for that, I'm going to get with my lawyer and have him start drafting the right paperwork to add your name on the deed. That'll fix you."

She enjoyed their banter. She hadn't played like this in years. "Until we come to the next topic of discussion," she said, grinning.

"I have one—namely when will you agree to be mine?"

Genevieve had no problem thinking of an answer because it was actually a critical one for her peace of mind. "The day I move in with you. Otherwise I *will* be losing clients due to my scandalous behavior."

After checking to make sure all three of her team would be at the office, Marshall drove Genevieve to town. Just seeing them enter together won giggles from Ina.

"Hello, Mr. Roark," she said shyly. "It's always good to see you."

"Make it Marshall, Ina, since you're going to be seeing a lot more of me from now on."

"So much for my wanting to break the news gently," Genevieve said with a wry smile.

Raenne came rushing out of the kitchen. "I heard that. Does that mean what I think it does? Show me the hand! Oh, my gosh—*Avery!* Get out here, *hasta la* giddyap and look at this ring!" The perky blonde grabbed Genevieve's left hand and all but salivated over the ring. "That's a stunner." Then she turned to mush. "Aw, congratulations, you two. We were all so worried it wouldn't happen."

Clearly determined to act more dignified, Avery emerged from her office at a more deliberate pace. "So you wore her down," she said to Marshall. "My money was on you."

"Have you set a day yet?" Ina asked.

"Not exactly," Genevieve told them. "But it's sooner rather than later."

"It better be. It's hard to get a good place for a reception around the holidays," Raenne said.

Genevieve shook her head, her expression growing impish. "That's not the only reason."

"Oh, my God," Avery groaned, narrowing her eyes as she studied her. "You aren't!"

"I am."

The usually cool and collected brunette grabbed her and hugged her. "Hallelujah and raise the flag!"

When Genevieve fought a gag, a startled Avery quickly backed off. "Jeez, Gen, I'm sorry. I didn't think I was that strong."

"Morning sickness," Marshall offered.

Slapping herself in the middle of the forehead, Avery muttered, "Of course!" She immediately began waving her arms around, her Dolman-sleeved jacket flapping like bird wings. "I make a motion," she declared to all. "From now on this is a scent-free zone!"

With one hand clamped to her mouth, Genevieve waved her thanks. "I'm sure it's just temporary."

The announcement went so well, Marshall encouraged Genevieve to move on to her mother's house. Bart answered the door not quite looking his upbeat self, but seeing them, he brightened.

"This is a nice surprise. Come in." He hugged Genevieve and kissed her on each cheek.

As he shook Marshall's hand, she asked, "Is Mother hard at work?"

"Not so much so that I can't take a break for my favorite child." Sydney announced, already descending the staircase.

She looked affluent and elegant in a rust pants

ensemble that looked very in keeping with the fall weather. As always, she jingled with every step like a belly dancer thanks to the various pieces of jewelry she was wearing.

"Gigi, darling, you're feeling better? You certainly look as though you are."

Genevieve accepted her mother's embrace, but did not smile. "I'm okay. I wasn't so okay when Marshall and I talked and we determined that your mouth triggered a great deal of pain for him—and me for that matter."

While Sydney held her right hand against her throat, Bart shot his wife a pained look. "I had the awful suspicion that you had something to do with Marshall leaving. They should name a hurricane or cyclone after you, Syd. You're long overdue."

Although she looked a bit uneasy at first, Sydney recovered well. "I don't know what you all are talking about. I've been nothing but supportive of them. And protective." She looked from Genevieve to Marshall. "Tell him."

Genevieve shook her head. "You never think of the ramifications of what you're saying. You don't know the meaning of the word *edit* outside of your work."

"I do so."

"You repeated part of our conversation at lunch last week," Genevieve told her. "When taken out of context, Marshall misunderstood. Added to other misperceptions…well, that's why he went away."

"No," Sydney replied, firm in her rejection. "That can't be. What did I say that could be possibly be misconstrued? I'm a writer, for pity's sake!"

"Stop while you're ahead and say 'sorry,'" Bart said,

looking a little less amused and tolerant than he usually was. "Just be grateful they figured things out and are together for good this time." He raised his eyebrows as he pointed an unlit pipe at Genevieve's left hand. "I take it that's the deal-maker?"

Looking shaken and more than a little uncomfortable, Sydney laughed thinly as she noticed Genevieve's ring. "Why, Marshall, you have excellent taste."

"No, my excellent taste is asking Genevieve to become my wife," Marshall said, slipping his arm around her waist. "She's agreed. I hope we have your blessing."

Genevieve held out her left hand to give them a better view of the ring. Bart wasted no time in hugging her, longer this time.

"Sweetheart, my prayers have been answered. I couldn't be happier for you," he said.

As he moved on to Marshall, Sydney approached her daughter. "I'm utterly ecstatic for you both." Casting her husband an apologetic look, she embraced Genevieve again. Then did the same to Marshall, although more awkwardly. "When is the big day?" she asked almost shyly. Her expression clearly indicated that she wasn't so sure about being invited.

Once again slipping his arm around Genevieve's waist, Marshall said, "We're narrowing down potential dates."

"And it will be very low-key," Genevieve added firmly. She cast Marshall a sidelong look. "Probably at Marshall's house."

"I'm putting that lawyer's number on speed dial," he murmured for her ears only.

"Oh, my dears." Sydney began rallying from her

short stay in hot water. "Please—have it here? And let me arrange for my portrait photographer to capture the moment. You'll want a memento for that precious child you're carrying."

Bart leaned to whisper in Genevieve's other ear, "She's relentless, isn't she?"

"There's no one like her," she replied with a fatalistic sigh.

"Sometimes I think I married the reincarnation of the Unsinkable Molly Brown."

Genevieve looked questioningly at Marshall. When he gave her a wink and nod, she said to her mother and Bart, "All right. Thank you, both."

"I think this calls for a Bloody Mary or mimosa," Bart declared.

It turned out that the wedding happened later, rather than sooner. And life got busier, and more complicated.

Only days later, Bart had a heart scare and was laid up in the hospital for several days before he was strong enough to undergo bypass surgery. Having experienced her second scare in such a short time, Sydney never left his side.

In the middle of October, only days after Bart returned home to convalesce from bypass surgery, Riley Butler suffered a stroke. He lingered for a day and passed away on his and Shirl's wedding anniversary.

With their son's gratitude, Genevieve helped Shirley move into an assisted-living facility. As close as they were, everyone expected she would soon follow Riley, and yet within days, Shirley Butler was playing dominos, cards and starting painting classes. She cut off the heavy braid that had been giving her headaches for years and got a perm. And Genevieve heard, the next time she went to check on her at the home, that she hadn't picked up a crocheting needle yet.

To celebrate Bart's continued convalescence, Sydney decided their growing family should have a traditional Thanksgiving meal at their residence. Bart grumbled the whole time for the single wine spritzer his wife limited him to and finally dumped the thing down the bar sink drain and poured himself a stout scotch-and-water.

Sydney went livid. "Fine—leave me a widow."

"I'll leave you a wealthy widow," he drawled, raising his glass to her.

Before the meal could turn into a cold war, Marshall stood. "I think this would be a good time to make a small presentation," he began. Then he turned to Genevieve and said, "You have their attention, my love."

She reached under the table and brought out a wrapped package they'd snuck in with the help of Dorothy. "As you know," she began, "we delayed our next appointment for my sonogram due to our darling St. Bart. But we finally did the procedure two days ago and here are the results." But before she handed it to them, she added beseechingly, "Look, you two. I know things have been tough and scary for you. But don't lose sight of why you two married. I love you. You're going to be the only grandparents our child has. I'm counting on you to establish lots of traditions like the one you're starting today."

With that she held out the box.

Sydney eagerly accepted it and had paper flying to the floor before Bart could join her at her end of the table.

She chipped a red polished nail prying off the lid and then swatted away the tissue paper. With Bart's hands on her shoulders as he lowered his head next to hers, she stared at the framed photo of Genevieve's ultrasound. As Bart began to grin, she lifted it from the box and held it higher as one would a baby.

"Oh, Bart," she said, her voice cracking. "We're going to have a grandson!"

Chapter Nine

"I hope that before the night is over, I don't end up wishing that we had eloped after all."

Hearing a hint of nerves in his bride-to-be's voice, Marshall backtracked to the bathroom and came behind Genevieve, where she stood before the master suite's vanity mirror. Gently grasping her by her shoulders, he kissed the back of her head and said, "Breathe, my love."

She had agreed to move in with him shortly after Bart's attack and Riley's death. Along with their desire to be together so they could share every moment of her pregnancy, it cut down on back-and-forth travel, and it let her be closer to Bart, whom she increasingly referred to as "Dad," much to Bart's delight.

But Marshall was as ready to finish getting this deed done and make her his wife, as she was to have this over. Genevieve—the woman who'd captured his imagination and given him back his sanity. His impulse was to sweep her into his arms and carry her two doors down with or without the necklace he'd bought her for this occasion. He was all but exploding from eagerness, although he'd been restraining himself and acting like the calm voice of reason for her sake. The last thing he wanted was to add to her stress. As good as she was getting at allowing herself to see him as partner and someone she could lean on, he knew her independence was only one old habit away. He wasn't going to risk some shadow of a doubt making her back out of this wedding in the last minute.

Calmly taking over, he swept the shining cape that was her golden hair over one shoulder and fastened the clasp of the starburst diamond pendant. It was as finely formed as she was as it rested in the subtle cleavage exposed by the square neck of her ivory gown. The cocktail-length velvet empire-style dress concealed the subtle swell of her abdomen. She'd been firm about being discreet for this occasion in respect for the minister of her church who had graciously agreed to perform the service.

"Thank you," she said with relief. "You have to promise to tell me if I start to sound even slightly high maintenance. I know what they say about daughters turning into their mothers, and I refuse to 'Sydney' you."

Chuckling dryly, Marshall added another kiss to the side of her neck—one of his many favorite spots on her body. "I actually think your mother is trying to turn over a new leaf or three by taking lessons from you. Bart confided in me the other day that he's never been prouder of her. She actually went golfing with him. Well, she stayed in the golf cart the whole time, but she went."

Genevieve gaped. "He didn't tell me. Neither did she."

"I think there was some romancing afterward and Sydney's probably afraid you'd make fun of her."

"I'd hug her neck for remembering she had a husband and not just an escort to social galas and a backup checkbook. Oh, I hope they continue to behave tonight."

"Genevieve, mine—" Marshall leaned over her shoulder to lean his cheek next to hers "—try to focus on what's about to happen. All I want is for you to enjoy this moment as much as I am. What are we looking at—two hours maximum before we can be alone again? We can handle that."

She met his gaze in the mirror, her left eyebrow arching as her skepticism surfaced. "That's wonderful in theory. But you know it's been three whole days since I've dealt with this nausea, and I'm so feeling the potential for it happening again. What if it comes back right at the moment Pastor Jarvis starts the vows?"

Taking the role of the pragmatic, he massaged her shoulders and stroked her arms to continue soothing her. "We'll be asking a half-dozen people to be patient. That's hardly the entire congregation at the Washington Cathedral—or your church for that matter." Having been at her side and witnessed all that she'd been through, he sympathized. "It's going to be fine, even if your mother is directing this. You probably also don't know that with her attempting to behave herself, Bart's been better at following his doctor's directives."

He knew, though, that she'd experienced several challenging weeks. Along with Bart's health issue and old Riley passing, she had lost two contracts, and not due to fair competition, either. She lost because two couples in her church were "offended" by her personal behavior that they claimed set a bad example for the community. He'd found it laughable how they—with seven children between them—could find love, enhanced by a healthy sexual attraction, offensive.

At least she'd been spared the crass disrespect of overhearing one of the painters he'd hired as they'd begun to prepare Genevieve's house to be put on the market. He happened to be arriving to check on things when the jerk—who was married, no less—made a disparaging remark about her new financial status as though she hadn't worked hard and successfully for every dollar she'd earned herself. However, what triggered Marshall's fury was the added comment that he wouldn't have turned down a chance in her bed any more than Marshall had. It had given Marshall great pleasure to personally remove the ingrate from the premises.

Those instances aside, it had been reassuring to see that most people who knew Genevieve and what she'd gone through with losing Adam were delighted for her and warmed quickly to him. Of course, it helped that he strongly supported local businesses and labor as he contracted work at both residences and helped Shirley's son find people to get the Butler house ready for Genevieve to list it for sale.

"You're right," she said. She swept her hair back behind her shoulders and nodded with resolve.

"You're the most beautiful bride a groom could imagine," he murmured.

"And you—" she turned to smooth her hands over his black suit "—are the most handsome groom."

"Ready?"

"Let's go."

Genevieve had stood firm against her mother's attempts to turn the wedding into a holiday party for the who's who in town. She'd insisted that she wanted the wedding to be about family. Of course, her "family" included the agency personnel.

When they arrived at the Sawyers' brightly lit Mediterranean mansion, Bart opened the door and pressed his hand to his heart. "Call the medics—I'm having the big one!"

Distressed, Genevieve scolded him. "Dad, don't joke about that."

"Sorry, sweetheart, but you are a vision. You look like a young queen at her coronation," he said and tenderly kissed her. "I'm so proud and happy for you."

"Oh, mercy, you're going to make me cry and ruin my makeup."

Laughing, he released her and, ignoring Marshall's outstretched hand, he hugged him enthusiastically. "Welcome to the family, old son."

Grinning, Marshall warned, "Thanks. Just don't rush the 'old' part."

The house was resplendent with holiday decorations. A fifteen-foot tree stood in the foyer before the grand staircase lit with the same white lights that framed the exterior of the house. The ornaments were in Sydney's favorite colors—red and gold. The banister was wrapped in faux pine garland enhanced with the same tiny lights, gold ornaments and red poinsettias. At least a dozen more poinsettias adorned side tables.

The tree in the living room was half the size and

decorated all in red with red lights. The fireplace mantel was enhanced with Sydney's collection of glass Christmas trees that she'd collected from all over the world. The coffee table hosted an array of ivory candles of various dimensions and shapes, while every window was framed in white lights that highlighted planters containing white and red poinsettias.

Avery, Raenne and Ina were in the middle of taking a tour of the room, champagne flutes in their hands. When Genevieve and Marshall entered, they rushed over to fuss over her and flirt with him.

"So gorgeous."

"Is that the necklace you gave her, Marshall? Wow!"

"Where's the baby bump?"

Avery's question had Genevieve stroking the little swell. "Discreetly hidden for the formal photos," she said wryly.

"Look, Marshall's wearing my tie I gave him at the wedding shower."

"Mr. Marshall, you'd look dreamy wearing one with the three little pigs all over it."

"Can I get a photo with you to send to my mother in New York? She thinks the reason I've given up on marriage is because I've turned gay."

Laughing again at irreverent Avery, Genevieve said, "Thank you for coming. It means so much to us. Raenne, didn't your husband want to join you? I can't believe he let you leave looking so pretty in that green satin."

"Thanks." Raenne wrinkled her nose. "Apparently I'm still not tempting enough to keep him from a bass tournament."

"Here?" Marshall was taken aback and felt sorry for her. "In December? On Christmas Eve?"

"Florida," Raenne said with a sigh. "Avery and I are heading for Dallas after this. We're going to spend the night in a swanky hotel and see what we can find in the way of 'ho-ho-ho.'"

"Please be safe," Genevieve said with concern.

"If we weren't going to be safe," Avery replied, winking at Raenne, "we would have gotten separate rooms."

Shaking her head, Genevieve asked Ina, "What are your plans? You always spend Christmas Eve with your children."

"We'll go to midnight mass, yes, and then a friend has invited us to his restaurant for a late Christmas Eve dinner."

"'His.' Did you hear that?" Raenne gasped. "Ina, you sly dog. Have you been holding out on us?"

The petite woman's dimples deepened as she smiled shyly. "I've been seeing Tomas Rivera for a few months."

"For Rivera's on the Interstate in Mt. Vernon?" Avery whistled. "Well done, *chica*."

The French doors leading to the dining room opened and Sydney emerged with the photographer. "I thought I'd heard your voices," she said. "Don't you think they make a stunning couple, Patrick? And I know with your talent, you're going to make it impossible to choose from among the proofs. Gigi, darling, Marshall, this is Patrick Jarvis, the only photographer I have been using ever since he did my jacket cover for my first *New York Times* hardcover."

"Perhaps since we have a little time I could get some photos of the bride," the handsome blond suggested, hardly able to take his eyes off Genevieve.

"Good idea." Stepping behind her, Marshall drew Genevieve against him, clearly reminding the younger man who she belonged to. "I'd like one for my office."

She covered his arms with hers. "And I'd like one of you for mine."

"Wait! Wait!" Dorothy came scurrying in from the kitchen like a frisky terrier. "I almost forgot to bring these out. Mrs. Sawyer and Mr. Bart wanted you to have this, dear." She handed Genevieve a branch bouquet of white orchids. "And this is for you, sir." She handed Marshall a white rose for his lapel.

"Let me." Genevieve handed the orchids to Ina, who was closest, and secured the boutonniere to his lapel with the hat pin that had been provided.

"Is white for eternity?" he asked softly, watching her.

"I don't think there's anything written in stone, but I like the thought. I'd also read it's for purity—as in purity of intent."

"Tonight is definitely that." Aware that they were the center of attention, and that the photographer was getting impatient, Marshall stepped aside and him get to work.

Patrick had finished with Genevieve and was starting on Marshall when the pastor arrived. The ceremony could begin.

The service took place in the foyer in front of the tree. Genevieve and Marshall held hands the whole time and hers were trembling. He held her gaze and soon the trembling stopped, as the world around them faded away.

Finally, they shared their first kiss as husband and wife. That was met with sighs, cheers and sighs by their small group of witnesses.

Marshall touched his forehead to Genevieve's. "Mrs. Roark."

Hugs and countless toasts followed. The two-tiered cake was cut and Patrick took his last picture. After that, Marshall reached into an inside jacket pocket and brought out an envelope that he had been holding for Genevieve.

She said to her friends and employees, "Since it's also Christmas, I wanted you to know how much I value you. Not only for covering for me when I was under the weather, and still maintaining our record in the region, but for setting such excellent and humbling examples of what loyalty and friendship means. This is a heartfelt token of my love and appreciation for you."

She handed Ina, Avery and Raenne each a smaller envelope from inside the original one. They all murmured their thanks and ripped them open with excitement. Then they went wide-eyed and silent as they saw the amounts of the checks.

"Oh, and don't worry," Genevieve added. "I paid the tax on that."

"Heavens," Ina whispered. "This is so generous."

"Darn it, Rae," Avery teased. "We should skip Dallas and book a flight to Paris."

Rae didn't laugh. In fact, she kept looking at Genevieve and Marshall and finally said, "You know, watching you two and seeing what you share has made me stop lying to myself. I don't need to hang on to a wedding band, lying to myself that it's a security blanket when I'm the income earner in the family. And it sure isn't a status symbol to prove I have a man. I'm going to open my own bank account with this check…and hire a lawyer."

While Avery raised her glass and said, "Amen," Genevieve embraced Raenne. Marshall could see the concern on her face, but relief, too.

Things wound down after that and soon Marshall drove his wife back to their home. "Feel any different?" he asked. He felt utterly at peace, and grateful.

"I'm not sure that I should," Genevieve replied, turning to watch his profile. "But I do. Do you?"

He nodded once. "Vows are powerful things. I always believed that. But I'm feeling the gift as well as the responsibility of them more the second time around."

"Exactly. It's like seeing the sun every day, and then there's a terrible storm. When the sun comes out again, you feel as though it's never looked more glorious."

Once Marshall parked in the garage and shut down the purring sedan, he exited and met her on the passenger side. "Want me to carry you inside?"

"Oh, you don't have to prove you're romantic, Mr. Roark." Genevieve leaned her head against his shoulder. "On any day, you show me countless times and ways. I hope Raenne finds this kind of happiness. I hope they all do."

"Ina seems to be on her way." Unlocking the door, Marshall took her hand and led her inside. "But enough about your flock of single ewes. I want to find out if making love with my wife is different than making love to my lover."

Genevieve had started laughing at his description of her friends, but when he voiced his intent, she stopped. Her eyes took on an invitation and promise that kicked his pulse up a notch.

"What would my husband like?" she asked, walking backward as she drew him through the house toward the master suite. "Joint massages with the warmed lotion you like so much, or a long soak in the Jacuzzi tub…?"

Marshall remembered their last adventure in massages and the images in his mind went straight to his groin. Then again, the thought of her lovely and glistening while being caressed by bubbles as well as himself was equally appealing. "We haven't broken in that tub yet, have we?"

When the water was the right depth, the temperature warmed to perfection, and the candles were lit, they helped each other undress and settled in. Marshall loved that she wasn't shy about being nude in front of him. He and Genevieve had been in tune with each other from that first time.

"What's putting that interesting smile on your face?" Genevieve asked from the other end of the tub.

"You." She looked exactly as he'd fantasized she would in here when he would walk through the house in those early days alone and yearning for her. She'd scooped up her hair with one of those long clip things that gave her that sexy dishabille look, her skin glowed from the warmth and humidity, as her eyes did with anticipation. Her cheeks were the color of her nipples tempting him as the frothing water gave him teasing glimpses. "Is this more comfortable for you than the shower?"

"There's a little more room." Her lips curved as she

tickled the inside of his thighs with her toes. "Our positions in here might be more compatible with being pregnant, but I've enjoyed our shower. Very much."

"Speaking of positions, what are you doing way over there? Come over here and talk to me."

Laughing softly, she rose on her knees and did as he'd invited, settling onto his lap. "Talk? Is that all you want me to do?"

With her breasts now above the moving water, Marshall took his time admiring and caressing her. He loved how she moved into his touch, then arched to give him more access. But under the water, her hands were busy, too, and that wreaked havoc on his concentration, let alone his intention to prolong this love play.

Suddenly he sucked in a short, sharp breath. "Do that again."

"Did I do something?" she asked, all innocence.

"Where has this mischievous streak been hiding?"

She abandoned his hard shaft to caress his chest and nip gently on his nipples. "As in *The Night Before Christmas,* it was tucked away for 'a long winter's nap.' I can behave," she whispered, rubbing her breasts against him and licking at the moisture on his neck and chin. "I wouldn't want you to regret marrying me."

"What I already regret is that I won't have a hundred years of this—and you." Taking hold of her hips, he urged her up. "Take me inside. Now."

She did and he closed his eyes in the poignant pleasure. Then when she tightened her inner muscles, it was all he could do not to lose control. "Stop, you delectable minx or you're not going to get much out of this ride."

"I'm patient, and we have all night."

When she tightened around him again, he wrapped his arms around her and held her fiercely against him until their hearts beat as one. "I love you so damned much."

Genevieve framed his face with her hands and kissed him softly. "Thank you for not giving up on me."

"God, how could I? You're my reason for bothering to breathe."

Taking hold of his hand, she brought it over the gentle swell of her abdomen. "You mean we are."

"Baby, baby," he crooned. Smiling, Marshall slid his hand downward to where they were joined, and caressed her with his thumb. "Let's ride, Mrs. Roark."

With a whimper of desire, Genevieve sought a deeper kiss and they raced to ecstasy together.

Epilogue

The following May...

"How about a massage?"

Genevieve didn't know whether to laugh or cry. "That cinches it, Mr. Roark. You break that rule that no one is irreplaceable. Here I look as though I swallowed the Dallas Cowboy stadium, I feel as though the entire team is practicing under this dome," she continued, stroking her very protruding belly, "and you're sweetly trying to make me feel sexy."

"Well, I hate to burst your pouty party bubble, my love, but you are. If Dr. Nyland hadn't told you that we need to behave for these last days, I'd already have you out of your clothes."

She'd just made it home from the office after showing a client who could not choose between the six houses

Genevieve had taken her to. The only reason she was back yet was due to Marshall watching the weather on TV. A spring storm was gearing up along a front about to move through the region. He'd called and urged her to call it a day and get home to safety.

He took her into his arms and stroked her back. "Thank you for coming home and not riding this system out at the office. I would have made myself sick with worry. Correction, I'd probably have wrecked the car or tried to get out of another speeding ticket from Phil Irvine racing to ride it out with you there."

"You can thank my swollen ankles and screaming back. I just couldn't take any more."

"Poor sweetheart. You've barely gained enough weight for this little guy." As the first flash of lightning and crack of thunder alerted them that things were about to get noisier and rougher on this second day of May, Marshall added, "Well, there goes my suggestion that we draw you a warm bath so you could unwind. It's too dangerous now."

"I'll settle for curling up under a throw. I'm so tired I'll bet I could nap through the noise."

"That would please me to no end. Go make yourself comfortable. But if you don't mind, come lie on the couch. If the tornado sirens go off, I want you close to the closet behind that big brick fireplace wall."

"They better not tease us with those noisy things," she said, easing out of her shoes and carrying them to their bedroom. "Once I lie down, it'll take a crane to move me."

Before Genevieve was fully changed into a pair of soft blue sweats, the lightning was almost constant and the thunder was shaking some of the windows. She was about to return to the living room when a particularly bright flash and crack—soon followed by a long booming sound—had her ducking. Only seconds later a sudden cramp had her bending in half, quite taking her breath away.

Oh, no.

She knew she had been feeling a bit achy and uncomfortable all day, but she figured it was the humid weather and the strains her client had put upon her out-of-shape body. But now she was increasingly unsure.

Before the next cramp started, she was crumpled on the throw rug beside the bed. When the worst of it passed, she tried to call Marshall's name, but the sirens sounded.

"That's it, Genevieve," he called from the other side of the house. "Let's get you settled."

She was as settled as she was going to get, she told him mentally. She withstood the last cramp and screamed, "Marshall!"

He came running and when he saw her, he swore. "What happened? Did you fall?"

"Hurt. Labor pains. I think I've been having them for a while, but I thought it was my icky lunch. Oh, God. My water just broke. We have to get to the hospital."

"Sweetheart, we can't," Marshall replied, reaching for her. "The weather radio says we're within five miles of a twister. We can't risk driving in those conditions." He kneeled beside her and kissed her reassuringly. "It'll be all right. We'll get this done."

Just then the lights went out.

After another gasp, Genevieve laughed at the irony

of things. "Sure," she said to the ceiling. "Make this easier."

Stroking her back, Marshall said, "It's not that dark. Our eyes just need to adjust. I'd open the drapes, but if it gets so bad there's flying debris, those heavy drapes might help protect us. Stay put. I'm going for candles, flashlights, a vinyl tablecloth—"

"Okay, but please hurry." It seemed a small eternity before he returned. By then she was finishing another cramp. Once he had the candles lit and the tablecloth situated beneath her, he called Dr. Nyland on his BlackBerry.

"Tell her this is Marshall Roark and my wife's water burst," he said to whoever had answered and didn't want to patch him through. While waiting, he kissed Genevieve on her damp forehead. "How are you doing, babe?"

"I'm not scared if that's what you're wondering. I know you won't panic."

"We have it under control. No need to panic. Nah, I won't panic." Another flash and instant, earsplitting blast of thunder had Marshall burying a shuddering Genevieve against his chest. "Jeez. There went the boathouse, I suspect."

"Or the roof. I hope Mother is keeping an eye out her window and checking for smoke here. I know the roof is fireproof, but what about—?"

Marshall held up his hand and said, "Yes, Doctor. That's right. How close? Damned fast considering all you suggested we read. She says she was probably having mild contractions all day. But this is her first baby, and you think that means a longer labor, right?" He made a face. "Yes, it being an honor aside, she'd prefer you deliver our child." He sighed. "Yes, Doctor, if we survive this tornado that's in the area, I'll put on my big-boy pants."

Genevieve choked and he winked at her.

"Here's Genevieve. Reassure her while I go get what else that I need."

Once he was out of earshot, Genevieve said, "Tracy, I can't believe you said that to him."

"Oh, he has a good sense of humor," Dr. Nyland replied. "It just doesn't stretch too far where you're concerned. You have a good man there."

"I know it. So now tell me again what to be prepared for. Wait—another contraction is starting."

By the time Marshall returned, the wind had picked up to gale force. Genevieve was doing the natural childbirth breathing with Dr. Nyland. Outside, something banged against the house.

"I don't care if that's another woman in labor trying to get inside," Marshall muttered. "We're booked solid."

Genevieve managed a pained smile. "Cute. Can you help me out of these sweats? Get my short terry robe from my closet. I'm going to have to nurse after you clear the baby's nose and mouth passages."

He hurried to the closet and did what she asked, then assisted her into changing into it. Helping her ease onto her side for a moment, he slipped on the new gloves he'd taken from a sealed bag. After that he kissed the inside of Genevieve's knee and checked to see if the baby's head was showing yet. "Oh, my God—he's got my hair!"

"Did you hear that, Tracy? Little Robert—*oh!*—has Marshall's hair—*oh!* I have to push."

And then it was happening. Genevieve thrust the BlackBerry at Marshall and rose up on her elbows.

"Push!" he rasped, his gaze zipping from hers to the tiny, dark head emerging from her.

Exhausted, Genevieve slumped back onto the pile of towels he'd placed for her to use instead of pillows.

"Catch your breath, my love. You're doing beautifully. I'm getting his mouth and nose clear. Are you listening, Doc? He's moved to his side naturally just as you said he would."

"Marshall, I need to push again," Genevieve groaned.

"Go ahead, darling. I have his head in my palm. Only when you're ready."

Genevieve was ready. Oh, she wanted this done and to hold her baby. She pushed hard and one little shoulder emerged.

"Don't pull," she warned him breathlessly.

"I remember, but I so want to. It's killing me to see you suffering."

"Hush. I have to push." And she did.

The rest of the baby emerged wet and slick like a little seal landing on a beach.

Marshall made sure his face was clear and grinned wide when the little one uttered a lusty cry. "You want your mommy. I understand completely."

He tenderly set the child onto Genevieve's chest. "Our son," he said, leaning over to kiss her gently. "Thank you, my heart."

"Oh, he's perfect," she whispered.

Marshall tied the shoelace he'd found in his closet between four and six inches down the umbilical cord above the baby's belly button. Then he helped Genevieve coax their son to her breast. Only then did he grab a washcloth and pick up the BlackBerry. "Hear that, Doc? Just waiting on the placenta. She's starting the contractions now. Is she amazing or what?"

Once the placenta was discharged and Marshall had tied it off, too, Genevieve reminded him to finish his job. "Cut the cord now." She'd been adamant on that even if they had given birth in the hospital. She'd loved the tales about the child having a special affinity with whoever did that.

When that was done, Marshall fell back against the bed and stared at his family with awe.

"You're crying," Genevieve said, reaching to brush his cheek. She had never loved him more.

New sirens sounded, bringing in the outside world. The all-safe signal. Dr. Nyland disconnected soon afterward, having informed them that the EMTs would be there at any moment and she would see them at the hospital.

The house phone started ringing before Marshall could get up to pull the drapes open and go unlock the front door. He looked at the display and said, "It's your mother."

"Hand me the receiver," Genevieve said. Once he did, she clicked the green phone and said, "Hi, Grandma... Yes, during the storm." There was a loud scream on the other end that had Genevieve moving the phone to arm's length. "You and Bart better get here quick before the EMTs take me away," she told her.

There was laughter and tears as the growing family looked on in wonder at their little miracle. The ambulance soon arrived and Marshall walked beside his wife and son as they wheeled her outside. The sky was clearer than ever, the sun was glorious, just as Genevieve had described to Marshall on their wedding night—but there was also a rainbow brilliant in the southeast.

"How are we ever going to tell him this story?" Marshall said as they reached the truck. He bent quickly to kiss her for the short time apart, while he followed in his car.

With one arm wrapped protectively around their son, Genevieve reached up with the other and stroked his cheek. "We'll tell him the truth—it started with a house."

* * * * *

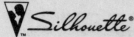
Silhouette®

COMING NEXT MONTH
Available September 28, 2010

SPECIAL EDITION

REQUEST YOUR FREE BOOKS!

2 FREE NOVELS PLUS 2 FREE GIFTS!

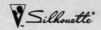

SPECIAL EDITION

Life, Love and Family!

*See below for a sneak peek at
our inspirational line, Love Inspired®.
Introducing HIS HOLIDAY BRIDE
by bestselling author Jillian Hart*

Autumn Granger gave her horse rein to slide toward the town's new sheriff.

"Hey, there." The man in a brand-new Stetson, black T-shirt, jeans and riding boots held up a hand in greeting. He stepped away from his four-wheel drive with "Sheriff" in black on the doors and waded through the grasses. "I'm new around here."

"I'm Autumn Granger."

"Nice to meet you, Miss Granger. I'm Ford Sherman, from Chicago." He knuckled back his hat, revealing the most handsome face she'd ever seen. Big blue eyes contrasted with his sun-tanned complexion.

"I'm guessing you haven't seen much open land. Out here, you've got to keep an eye on cows or they're going to tear your vehicle apart."

"What?" He whipped around. Sure enough, mammoth black-and-white creatures had started to gnaw on his four-wheel drive. They clustered like a mob, mouths and tongues and teeth bent on destruction. One cow tried to pry the wiper off the windshield, another chewed on the side mirror. Several leaned through the open window, licking the seats.

"Move along, little dogie." He didn't know the first thing about cattle.

The entire herd swiveled their heads to study him curiously. Not a single hoof shifted. The animals soon returned to chewing, licking, digging through his possessions.

Autumn laughed, a warm and wonderful sound. "Thanks,

I needed that." She then pulled a bag from behind her saddle and waved it at the cows. "Look what I have, guys. Cookies."

Cows swung in her direction, and dozens of liquid brown eyes brightened with cookie hopes. As she circled the car, the cattle bounded after her. The earth shook with the force of their powerful hooves.

"Next time, you're on your own, city boy." She tipped her hat. The cowgirl stayed on his mind, the sweetest thing he had ever seen.

*Will Ford be able to stick it out in the country
to find out more about Autumn?
Find out in HIS HOLIDAY BRIDE
by bestselling author Jillian Hart,
available in October 2010
only from Love Inspired®.*